MW01633477

A Duke's Daughters –
The Elbury Bouquet - Book 8 - Thorne

Clean Regency Romance

A HEART FOR AN HEIR

Arietta Richmond

USA Today Bestselling Author

Dreamstone Publishing © 2023

www.dreamstonepublishing.com

ISBN: 978-1-922735-16-4

DISCLAIMER

This is a work of fiction. Names, characters, places, organisations, events, and incidents are either products of the author's imagination or used fictitiously.

DEDICATION

For everyone who had the grace to be patient (and with this particular book, you've been very, very patient!) while this book, and every other book that I have written, was coming into existence, who provided cups of tea, and food, when the writing would not let me go, and endured countless times being asked for opinions.

For the readers who inspire me to continue writing, by buying my books! Especially for those of you who have taken the time to email me, or to leave reviews, and tell me what you love about my books, and what you'd like to see more of – thank you – I'm listening. I hope that you enjoy this new series (which features some appearances by old favourite characters from the His Majesty's Hounds series), just as much as my other books.

For my growing team of beta readers and advance reviewers – it's thanks to you that others can enjoy these books in the best presentation possible!

And for all the writers of Regency Historical Romance, whose books I read, who inspired me to write in this fascinating period.

TABLE OF CONTENTS

Books by Arietta Richmond

His Majesty's Hounds

Claiming the Heart of a Duke

Giving a Heart of Lace

Enchanting the Duke

Finding the Duke's Heir

Healing Lord Barton

Loving the Bitter Baron

Rescuing the Countess

Attracting the Spymaster

Intriguing the Viscount

Being Lady Harriet's Hero

Redeeming the Marquess

Winning the Merchant Earl

Kissing the Duke of Hearts

Falling for the Earl

Betting on a Lady's Heart

Courting a Spinster for Christmas

Restoring the Earl's Honour

A Scandalous Spring (An additional short story)

The Scent of First Love (an additional short story)

From Soldier Spy to Lord (contains the first three books in one volume)

To Love a Determined Lady (Contains Books 4, 5 and 6 in one volume)

Love Heals a Lord (Contains Books 7, 8 and 9 in one volume)

To Love a Dashing Lord (Contains Books 10, 11, 12, and 13 in one volume)

For a Lady's Honour (Contains Books 14, 15, 16, and 17 in one volume)

A Duke's Daughters – The Elbury Bouquet

A Spinster for a Spy (Lily)

A Bluestocking for a Baron (Rose)

A Minx for a Merchant (Primrose)

A Maiden for a Marquess (Iris)

A Vixen for a Viscount (Hyacinth)

A Diamond for a Duke (Camellia)

An Enchantress for an Earl (Violet)

A Heart for an Heir (Thorne)

The Family Sagas Collections

The Barrington Saga

The Morton Saga

The Dartworth Saga

The Edgeworth Saga

The Windemere Saga

The Chester Saga

The Nettlefold Chronicles

The Duke and the Spinster

A Duke in Autumn

To Wed an Earl

To Dance with the Dangerous Duke

A Christmas Bride for the Duke

The Marquess Elopes

The Scandalous Countess

Lady Canterford's Conspirators (The Mayfair Ladies Poetry Society)

A six book series (coming soon)

The Duke of Traithewood's Legacy

The Marquess Marries a Twin

The Regency Gothic Series

Lord of the Storm
Lord of the Shadows
Lord of the Darkness
Lord of the Lost

The Regency Scandals Series

The Gift of a Christmas Scandal
Christmas with *That* Duke
Lady Mariel's Scandalous Love
Lord of Dragons (written with Kyrii Rayne)

The Derbyshire Set

A Gift of Love (Prequel short story)
A Devil's Bargain (Prequel short story - coming soon)
The Earl's Unexpected Bride
The Captain's Compromised Heiress
The Viscount's Unsuitable Affair
The Count's Impetuous Seduction
The Rake's Unlikely Redemption
The Marquess' Scandalous Mistress
The Marchioness' Second Chance
A Viscount's Reluctant Passion
Lady Theodora's Christmas Wish
A Remembered Face (Bonus short story – coming soon)
The Duke's Improper Love (coming soon)
A Gentleman's Unconventional Courtship (coming soon)
The Derbyshire Set, Omnibus Edition, Volume 1 (the first three books in one volume.)
The Derbyshire Set, Omnibus Edition, Volume 2 (the second three books in one volume.)

Themed Collections

The Regency Christmas Hearts Collection
The Regency Christmas Love Collection
The Regency Spring and Valentine's Hearts Collection
The Regency Summer Hearts Collection
The Regency Autumn Hearts Collection
The Regency Spring Love Collection
The Regency Summer Love collection

The 'Her Duke' Collection

Her Summer Duke
Her Passionate Duke
Her Absent Duke
Her Determined Duke
Her Generous Duke
Her Christmas Duke

Other Books

The Scottish Governess
The Duke's Christmas Vow
Lady Augusta's Letters
The Crew of the Seadragon's Soul Series, (coming soon - a set of 10 linked novels)

ARIETTA RICHMOND

x

CHAPTER ONE

Thorne Gardenbrook, Marquess of Wildenhall, stared out of the Elbury House parlour window at the perfect April afternoon. It irritated him unreasonably.

The house was too quiet, now that all of his sisters were married and gone off to live their own lives, and he was left without an easy distraction. Growing up with seven younger sisters had kept him busy – teasing them, protecting them, escorting them about London and more. But now... it had been nearly two months since Iris' wedding, and his ability to entertain himself was proving to be minimal.

And if his mother hinted, one more time, that now the girls were all married, it was his turn...

He spun away from the window. He would go out, perhaps ride in Hyde Park...

Fifteen minutes later, when he came back down, changed into attire suitable for riding, he was very glad that he had made that choice.

"Thorne! I wanted to talk to you..."

"Sorry Mother – perhaps when I return? I should be back in time for dinner."

The Duchess huffed in annoyance, then shrugged, well aware that he was just as stubborn as she was, despite the fact that the impression he gave to the world was one of cheerful good humour.

"I will take that as a promise, and hold you to it. Enjoy your afternoon."

He sketched a rather impertinent bow, and went towards the back of the house and the door which led to the kitchen garden, and beyond that, the stables.

<<<<<O>>>>>

He reached Hyde Park before the most popular time for the *ton* to be there, and allowed himself the luxury of riding far faster than was truly acceptable in the Park. The rush of air past his face seemed to clear away his irritation with the world, and he soon slowed to a steady trot, allowing his horse to cool down after the run. He chose to ride away from the main paths, winding through the trees, and in and out of small clearings near the river.

At one point, as he came out of the trees, he saw a man on the opposite bank – a man engaged in exercise, it seemed. The gentleman had shed his coat, hanging it upon a branch, and was just finishing a set of movements involving a sword, which glittered in the sun as he moved. Thorne halted and watched, fascinated by the precision which was so effortlessly brought to the movements.

Eventually, the man stopped, coming to a stillness as precise as the movements had been, then, without fuss, he lifted something from the grass near the tree where his coat hung, and slid the sword into it. At first, Thorne thought it a scabbard, until the man set it down again, pulled his coat on, lifted it, and walked away.

In that instant, he realised that what had been a sword was now an innocuous looking cane.

A sword cane.

An idea arrived in his mind, whole and complete, without any warning – he would go to Mr Thomas Black's shop, and purchase himself a sword cane, then, next time he saw him, he would ask Blackwater to teach him to use it. Not that Thorne couldn't wield a sword... but Damien, his brother-in-law, was infinitely better at it than he was, and had much practice with sword canes in particular.

That would give him something to do, and something his mother likely would not interrupt.

He turned his horse, and set off at a steady slow canter, winding through the trees, back towards the Park gates, and the streets of London beyond.

<<<<<O>>>>

Lady Faith St John studied herself in the mirror. Wearing colours again was delightful, after the months of mourning for King George III. But was *she* delightful? She was beginning to suspect that she very much wasn't. This was her second Season, the first having been rather later than ordinary due to her father's and then her elder brother's deaths, and affected by scandal not of her making.

And most of this Season had been overshadowed by the mourning for the King's death. And now, she was twenty-one – tantamount to a spinster in the eyes of the *ton*. Some gentlemen had shown interest, it was true – but they were mainly the gamblers who found her dowry more attractive than anything else.

Perhaps tonight would be better, now that the mourning was finished – perhaps someone interesting would be there, someone new. Shaking her head, she laughed softly. There was no point deluding herself – the possibility of her making a good match was becoming vanishingly small. But... she refused, absolutely refused, to consider marrying one of the gamblers, or one of the men who cared nothing for her mind, and everything for her breasts, and more.

Rejecting the advances of men like that was becoming a sadly more frequent requirement, as they assumed that her approaching spinsterhood would make her desperate, and willing to accept them. Which she was not. Although desperate was beginning to be an accurate description…

She picked up her book, and went down to the parlour – perhaps an afternoon reading would put her in a better frame of mind.

<<<<O>>>>

The shopfront of Bentick and Black, Gentlemen's Outfitters, was plain yet boasted an elegant sign, recently redone with gilded letters. The street it was found on was respectable, if not in the first stare of fashion, as far as a location to shop.

Thorne rode along the street towards it, slowly, looking about for an urchin to hold his horse – surely, here, where there were shops, there would also be urchins looking to earn a coin. That assumption proved correct, and a boy slipped out of a narrow lane, and called to him.

" 'old yer 'orse, milord?"

"Yes. I'll be going into Bentick and Black." Thorne swung down, and pulled out a coin, handing it to the boy. "There's another of those for you, when I come out, so long as all is well with my horse."

The boy took the coin, and examined it, eyes glowing – a shilling was far more than the service warranted, but Thorne saw no reason not to be charitable.

"Yes, milord!"

He passed the boy the reins, and turned his attention to the shop. As he did, the door opened, and a woman stepped out, a cloak wrapped around her. She pulled the door closed behind her, and that movement opened the cloak for a short while – long enough for Thorne to see her tuck a package into her pockets, before she set off away from him, down the street, at some speed.

Most curious.

What was a woman doing coming out of a Gentlemen's Outfitters? And why was she swaddled in a large cloak, when the day was warm, even for late April? And, most curious of all, what was in the package that she had so swiftly tucked away?

He shook his head. It was none of his business, and he should forget about it entirely, but still…

Thorne strode to the door and opened it, causing a tinkle of small bells.

He stopped for a moment, blinking in the relative dimness after the bright sun outside.

"Can I help you, my Lord?"

Thorne went to where a man stood behind the counter. His uncanny resemblance to Blackwater still shook Thorne, even though he had now seen him a number of times.

"Mr Black, I have come to commission a sword cane from you. I believe that it is time I learnt to use one. I am told that they are quite different to a fencing rapier."

The man looked at him, now seeing him clearly in the beam of sunlight which shone through the large front window.

"Ah, my Lord… Wildenhall, isn't it?"

"Yes – I did not expect you to recognise me."

Mr Black laughed.

"I regard it as a matter of importance to memorise the names and appearance of all those in my half-brother's wife's family. I would not wish to embarrass Blackwater by getting such things wrong."

"I see. Well – what must we do, for you to make me a suitable sword cane?"

Mr Black came out from behind the counter, and led Thorne to the back of the shop area, where a rack of canes filled one wall.

"We will see which of these feels best to you, for your arm length, and the balance of it, then I will be able to define the exact specifications of what I must craft for you."

An hour passed, in which Thorne learnt more of swords and canes than he had ever expected to, and found it surprisingly interesting.

Then, they spoke of the price, and the time required for it to be made, and came to an agreement. Thorne, always conscious of how many of the *ton* did not pay tradesmen well, wrote a bank draft for half of the sum agreed immediately, and passed it to Mr Black.

"Thank you, my Lord. I do appreciate those who pay without being chased for it."

"I quite consciously choose not to be like many of my peers, on matters such as this."

Mr Black bowed, then tucked the bank draft away.

"Will there be anything else, my Lord?"

Thorne went to say no, to leave, but then the image of the woman leaving the shop rose in his mind, and curiosity drove him.

"Mr Black... as I came in, I saw a woman leave this shop, tucking something away. I admit to curiosity – why would a woman, wrapped in a cloak as if for concealment, be visiting a Gentlemen's Outfitters?"

Mr Black regarded him for some time, and Thorne wondered if he had offended the man. But then Black nodded, as if coming to a decision.

"I believe I'll tell you the truth of it, my Lord, for your family have proven to be trustworthy. I make and sell more than sword canes, as you know, but some of what I make is never seen in this shopfront. If you'll forgive me for it, I'll be blunt. I'm bastard-born – my mother at least did what she did out of love, however misplaced, but there are many women who end up with child, and not by willing choice, and many bastard-born children whose lives are far worse than mine has been. I want to give women a choice, a way to defend themselves."

Thorne contemplated those words - he could certainly agree with the sentiment.

"But… how?"

"Two ways, my Lord. With the weapons I make for them – knives disguised as those small tubes that women keep knitting needles and scissors in, for sewing, and other similar items that can fit in a reticule or a pocket – and by the things I teach them, about how to… fight dirty… shall we say, when a man attempts to do things they don't want."

"That's… a wonderful idea! When my sisters were younger, as they got closer to the age when men noticed them, I taught each one of them just where to apply a knee, or the heel of a boot, to… discourage… an overenthusiastic gentleman. One or two of them even used that knowledge to good effect a few times. But where do you do this? And how do you find the time?"

"That's the rub, my Lord. There really isn't enough time, since Blackwater acknowledged me, and the *ton* decided that they like my work. And there isn't really enough space here, either…"

Thorne stared at the counter top, unseeing, his mind turning it all over. He needed something to do, and something worthwhile – he refused to just drink and gamble his life away. He had funds – and he knew that Mr Black did too, now. What if… they could work together, and find a nearby building to buy, for just this purpose?

"Mr Black, does the idea of founding a personal defence school for women of the lower classes appeal to you?"

"Of course, my Lord, it's what I've been working towards – but… the time, and the finding of a place…"

"Mr Black, are you willing to take a partner in this venture? Because I have time, and I have funds to contribute."

Mr Black half gasped.

"You'd involve yourself in such a thing? You, a Duke's heir?"

"A Duke's heir with not enough to do, and a desire to help women – having seven sisters will make you think like that. For that matter, if I could think of a way to create a personal defence school for young women of the *ton* as well, I would. But how any of them might escape their mamas to attend I cannot, at this point, imagine."

"You've the right of it there, my Lord. But perhaps, if we start with the commoners, you'll come up with an idea, later…"

"By that statement, I take it that you'll have me as a partner in this endeavour?"

"Indeed – I'd be a fool to turn you away."

"Excellent! While you set to making my sword cane, I will set about finding us a building – close enough to here for convenience, and inconspicuous enough that the women coming to it will feel safe."

<<<<<O>>>>>

Marion, Countess of Hungerwood, spluttered, nearly dropping her teacup.

"Faith! You did what?!"

"I applied my knee to Lord Parrington's privates, with some considerable force. He released me with pleasing alacrity. I left him curled up on the terrace tiles, moaning piteously. It was entirely his own fault for attempting to continue when I had said no."

"Oh dear! No wonder he looked so very unwell when he came back into the ballroom. But was that wise? Will not that action likely make all men, good or bad, avoid your company? Men are, after all, quite sensitive about such treatment…"

Lady Faith St John sipped her own tea, and smiled, despite the fact that Marion's words sent a tiny frisson of fear through her.

"If they are afraid that I might do such a thing to them, then I can only assume that they would consider doing something to deserve it. And if that is the case, then I do not wish to know them."

"That is a valid point. We will just have to see if Parrington spreads gossip, or if he is too embarrassed to admit that he was felled so by a 'slip of a girl'."

"Perhaps we would all be better off if more young women of the *ton* knew how to do such things, how to defend themselves from unwanted amorous advances."

"Perhaps we would, indeed."

Faith nodded, and they went on to talk of other things, until Marion departed to visit her previous parents-in-law. Faith went out into the hall, intending to go up to her rooms, only to be stopped by one of the maids.

"My Lady, if I could speak to you for a moment?"

"Of course, Janie."

Faith regarded the maid curiously, and stepped back into the parlour with her.

"My Lady, did you really apply your knee to a gentleman's privates? At a Ball???"

"I did, and very effective it was."

"I'm sorry for eavesdropping, my Lady, but when I heard you say that, as I passed the door, I stopped, shocked. But what really caught my attention was when you said it would be better if more young women knew how to defend themselves. My Lady... some of us have been learning a bit about that. My cousin, who works at Lady Cobbett's, heard about it first and she told me. There's a man who owns a shop – he's been making ladies weapons for commoner women like me, and teaching them how to use them. It's a pity no one does that for the ladies of the *ton* – although perhaps the ladies of the *ton* don't need to defend themselves so often as we do?"

Faith laughed, shaking her head.

"Sadly, I think that the ladies of the *ton* have almost as much unwanted attention to deal with as any other woman – however, we at least sometimes have powerful relatives to help us. But… tell me more about this man and his shop. What sort of weapons does he make for ladies?"

Janie glanced around, as if worried that someone would overhear, or see them, then reached into the large pockets of her skirts, and pulled out a tube, made of leather. It looked like one of those things that ladies kept sewing or knitting implements in. Faith eyed it curiously.

"Like this, my Lady. If I open the lid here, it has a space for needles and the like, just as you'd expect, but if I then push this little button inside…"

Janie demonstrated, and part of the interior of the case popped up. Janie grasped it, and pulled, producing a wickedly sharp small dagger.

"Oh my! That would make most men pause, I should think."

Janie nodded.

"It certainly made that odious groom from next door pause, when he thought to kiss me in the lane."

Faith studied the maid for a moment, her mind full of questions and ideas. And hope – for if someone was making this possible for the maids and women of the streets, then perhaps it would be possible for women of the aristocracy too.

"Tell me, who is this man, and where is his shop?"

CHAPTER TWO

Mr Barlow Winthorpe paused on the front step of number thirty-six Sackville Street, in the act of inserting his key in the door. His attention had been caught by the carriage drawn up outside number thirteen, across the way, and a little further towards the middle of the run of the street. It appeared to bear a ducal crest, and he ground his teeth in annoyance at the sight.

To think that, after the Winthorpe Emporium having been in his family for hundreds of years, and at this very location for more than 80 years, he should be losing business to that disreputable upstart! Bentick had been a thorn in his side, and his father's before him, since he'd opened the shop at number thirteen thirty-five years ago, and had become more so when he'd taken on Thomas Black as a partner.

Barlow had hoped that when Bentick died, all would settle, but instead, that illegitimate, unseemly nuisance, Thomas Black, had had the indecency to continue the business, then to be revealed as the bastard son of a Duke. And worse than that, his half-brother, the current Duke, had acknowledged him, in front of all society! Which had resulted in half of Barlow's customers deciding to buy from Bentick and Black instead. Even the front of the building at number thirteen was unseemly, there having been installed two large glass windows, to allow for the obvious display of goods!

A man came out of Bentick and Black, stepped into the carriage, and was driven away as Barlow watched. Only once the carriage had turned at the end of the street and disappeared down Piccadilly did he turn back to the door and let himself in to his house, past the elegant bronze plaque which discreetly proclaimed this to be the business premises of the Winthorpe Emporium.

In the house next door, an aristocratic nose peeked around the edge of a curtain for a moment, then the woman turned away with a sniff of disdain. She, the aging spinster daughter of an Earl, regarded Mr Barlow Winthorpe with as much, if not more, disgust than Barlow regarded his competitors across the street. To think that she had to live next door to a man engaged in trade! Still, there had been times when seeing who came to his door had provided her with some rather delicious snippets of gossip…

<<<<O>>>>

Thorne had spent some days thinking about his conversation with Thomas Black, and exactly what would need to be done to put their plan into action. The whole concept had captured him, far more than anything else he had done or considered in years – he wanted to make it happen. He had spent so much time in thought, that he had apparently caused his mother great concern, as he discovered when she entered the parlour, and her voice jolted him out of his reverie.

"Wildenhall! What on earth is the matter with you? You've spent days looking shockingly serious, deep in thought, without laughing once. That is so utterly unlike you that I worry for your health. You aren't sickening for something, are you?"

He turned, somewhat startled by his mother's summation of his last few days, but had to admit that, on reflection, she had spoken accurately.

"No, no, Mother, I am quite well, I assure you. I've just been thinking, considering what I should do with my life."

Her eyes fixed him in place, pinning him rather like an insect to a board, ready for her very careful examination.

"You must definitely be sickening. You have actively avoided thinking about what to do with your life for the last ten years! Do you really expect me to believe that you are contemplating such things now? And if, by some slim chance, you actually are, do I dare hope that your contemplation includes the concept of which young lady you might marry?"

At that, Thorne did laugh.

"No Mother, not at this point, but I am sure that I'll get to that matter eventually."

His mother sighed, shaking her head.

"I really do despair of you! You know that you need an heir, for you will be Duke one day, and the continuance of the title must be ensured."

"I am fully aware of that Mother…"

She threw her hands in the air, and left the room. Thorne watched her go, a little sadly. Although he would never admit it to her, he had actually thought about the matter of who he might marry – many times, each with the same depressing result. He could not imagine spending his life with any of the young women he knew.

To shake off that gloomy thought, he decided to act. He would go out and ride, taking a winding path, so that he could traverse Sackville Street from end to end, and then Swallow Street – what remained of it after the building of the Quadrant – and assess which buildings might perhaps suit the purpose of his new project with Thomas Black. After that, he would continue his ride down Piccadilly, and through Green Park to Hyde Park. The ride would brighten his day, and serve a practical purpose at the same time.

An hour later, he set off, and found himself looking at every house he passed, considering how varied they were, and wondering just what features they would need in a property suitable for the school they wished to establish. He had not, previously, ever really thought much about the various constructions of house, and the rooms they contained.

Oddly, the idea of investigating such things appealed to him – it was far more interesting than most of the other things he might do – the things that most of the men his age went and did. He had never been one for gambling, or boxing, or horseracing, although he liked to keep himself in good physical condition through riding, fencing, and the like.

Once he reached Sackville Street, he rode slowly along it, from north to south, studying the buildings as he never had before. The street was an odd mix of business and private residences – the houses had, it appeared, all originally been built as residences, but, over the years, a number had been modified, like Mr Black's, to have shopfront windows at ground level, yet retain the use as a residence in the upper floors.

There were more like that on the same side of the street as Bentick and Black than the other – Thorne wondered why. Putting that consideration aside for now, he turned the corner left into Piccadilly, and then went left again into Swallow Street. He was familiar with the house that Lady Prunella Danby now occupied, which Mr Black owned, but he had not really given much thought to the rest of the street. There was the church of course, and its associated buildings, but as he rode north along the narrow street, he realised that, in the last four years, the street had changed dramatically.

In that four years, the Quadrant on Regent Street had been built – and building it had involved the destruction of most of the buildings which had been in the northern section of that block of Swallow Street. Where once the street had continued, a narrow lane now led into a tangle of what was left of buildings, stables, and the like, trapped between the rear of the houses on Sackville Street, and the high walls of the rear of the buildings which made up that part of the curve of the Quadrant. Opposite that, another narrow lane led through under the upper storey of the Quadrant buildings, and out onto Regent Street.

Thorne rode through there, then went left, and up Regent Street to then turn left into Vigo Lane at the end of the Quadrant buildings. And there, at the end, between Regent Street and Sackville Street, was an entryway to a large livery stables, just before the corner house. He turned into Sackville Street again, and studied the first houses in from the corner.

An idea was beginning to form, and, to his delight, he noticed a small sign at the front of number twenty-three and number twenty-four, which declared that those buildings were for sale, and gave the name of a solicitors firm to contact. Thorne swung down from his horse, and pulled a small journal and a pencil from an inner pocket, so that he might take down the details.

Once that was done, he stood there for a few minutes longer, looking closely at the houses before him. They looked unassumingly respectable, rather like the rest of the street – which was just what he wanted, especially as this street contained the residences of a number of titled or important people. But what mattered most wasn't what they looked like at the street front – it was, instead, what was behind them, and how accessible that space was... A property like this might enable them to take their endeavour, should it succeed with the servant women, also to the young ladies of the *ton*.

Smiling, he tucked the pencil and journal away, swung back onto his horse, and set off for Green Park.

<<<<O>>>>

For days, Faith had been unable to think of anything other than the secret dagger which the maid, Janie, had revealed to her. Everything about that conversation echoed through her mind – the possibilities were just so far reaching! The idea that any man cared enough about the fate of common women to make things like that was astounding, and that he did so for virtually no cost was even more remarkable. Add to that the fact that he then taught the women how to use the weapons he provided...

She had to meet this paragon. No matter who he was, or what his background was, he had to be a man she could respect... and learn from. That last was uppermost in her mind. She would very much like to have a deadly little weapon like that in her reticule, and to be sure that she knew how to use it to best effect. Just imagining Lord Parrington's expression should she confront him with a dagger was rather satisfying.

On this day, she had woken far earlier than usual, after dreaming of daggers and swords, and now lay in bed attempting to decide what to do, for there was no chance that she would manage to get back to sleep. After a few moments of contemplation, she admitted to herself that she already knew what she wanted to do – it was just a matter of doing it.

It was a decision which would require Janie's cooperation, and would involve doing things which were decidedly improper – but Faith had always been far happier doing things which bounded on the edge of impropriety than at any other time. Being a 'proper young Lady' was unmitigatedly dull, in her opinion. She almost laughed at that thought, for she could imagine her mother shaking her head in frustration, as she so often had in the past.

Admitting to herself that she'd already decided galvanised her into action, and she slipped from her bed, going straight to her dressing room. Rather than ring for Meg to help her dress, she dressed herself in a plain round gown – it was quite suitable for walking about the house, especially when no one else but the servants was likely to be awake, and had the advantage of being something she needed no help with.

Ten minutes later, she slipped down the stairs, and went in search of Janie. The footman in the hall looked startled as she passed him, but said nothing when she went by without asking for any assistance. It took six rooms before she discovered Janie, who had just finished filling the coal scuttles in all of the lower rooms.

"Janie…"

The maid jumped, startled, not having heard her come into the room.

"Oh! My Lady, I didn't hear you…"

"I'm sorry – I didn't mean to surprise you so. But I did want to talk to you. Can you pause for a few minutes?"

Janie appeared to think, then nodded.

"Yes. I can stop for a short while now, and still get everything done."

"Excellent!"

She shut the door behind her, and went across the room to Janie, who was looking rather nervous.

"What did you want to talk to me about, My Lady? Is there something I've done…?"

Faith shook her head.

"No, no, no! You have done nothing wrong, never fear. It's just… I've been thinking about what you told me – about the man who makes those little hidden daggers, and teaches women how to use them. I've decided that I want to go to his shop, to meet him, and maybe to get something like that for myself. I want you to help me do it, for I don't want my mother or my brother and his wife to know about it. Which means taking a cab, and dressing to camouflage myself. I'd feel better if you went with me – you've been there before, after all."

"But… by yourself? That's… not something a young Lady of your class should do, surely?"

"Exactly – which is why I need your help. Will you do it? We will need to work out a time, and then you can tell the housekeeper that I have asked you to run an errand for me – that will be almost true, and she's unlikely to question it."

Janie paled a little, then nodded.

"All right, my Lady, I'll do it. I might still get into trouble if we're found out, but I think it's a good idea for you to be able to protect yourself if you need to… one of my cousins is a jarvey – has his own cab and all – should I get him to take us, when we go?"

"Oh yes! Thank you! I will work out when I might be able to get away without it being noticed, and then we can make arrangements."

With that, Faith slipped out of the room, leaving Janie to get back to her work. No one noticed her as she went back to her rooms, except the same footman, who looked the other way, and minutes later she was back in her nightrail, and back in bed. She didn't ring for Meg for a full half hour after that.

<<<<O>>>>

The man behind the desk had risen as Thorne was shown into the room, and bowed respectfully.

"Lord Wildenhall – what can I assist you with today?"

"My sister, the Duchess of Blackwater, Mr Thomas Black, and quite a few other people have informed me that you are a most efficient man-of-business, and that you are very good at managing... unusual... requests."

"I see. Please do be seated, my Lord, and tell me more about your particular 'unusual request' – for I assume that you have one?"

Thorne gave a short laugh, finding himself liking this man, whose sober attire and manner was offset by a decided twinkle in his eye, as if he enjoyed the opportunity to tackle work which was out of the ordinary.

"I do indeed. I have a reputation for being a rather light hearted fellow, but I find that, now all of my sisters are married, I am lacking in entertainment – with the size of our family, just being in our home used to be enough to keep me amused – as a result, I now seek other things to put my time to. I have never been given to gambling or excessive carousing, and there are few other entertainments for young men."

"I agree – you are wise not to gamble and drink your life away."

Thorne watched as curiosity rose in Mr Swithin's eyes. He nodded, and went on, coming to the important part of this meeting.

"Quite by accident, I saw something which caused me to develop an interest in learning to use a sword cane – which led me to the shop door of Bentick and Black, of course. But what I saw as I went to enter the shop was unusual, so I asked Mr Black about it. The conversation which followed provided me with a far more intriguing new enterprise with which to fill my days."

Mr Swithin was by now almost quivering with interest, and Thorne knew that he was teasing the man unmercifully, by taking so long to get to the real point of the matter.

"And that enterprise somehow requires my services?"

"Indeed, Mr Swithin, it does. That enterprise, which I will undertake in partnership with Mr Black, is an expansion of something that he has been doing, as a matter of charity, for some time now. He has been making something which is an idea that came to him as a result of sword canes, but which is far smaller. He has been creating those little tubes which ladies carry knitting and sewing implements in, but creating them in a manner which also houses a hidden dagger. A miniature sword cane for women, of a sort. And he has been selling them, for a pittance, to the maids who work in the houses of the nobility, so that they have a way to defend themselves from unwanted advances." Mr Swithin had developed a distinct smile, and Thorne felt a rush of relief fill him – he had wondered how the man might react for, after all, arming lower class women was a rather scandalous concept. "And to make sure that they get value from those daggers, he has been teaching them the basic tenets of knife fighting."

"I must say, I heartily approve, no matter that such a sentiment puts me at odds with most of the men of the aristocracy, I am sure. But... what does this enterprise need from me? And what is your involvement?"

"When Thomas told me of it, my first thought was that such items and lessons should be available to all young women – not only maids, but the young ladies of the *ton* as well. I asked if he had considered that, and he said he had, but both funds and time limited him. So I decided to invest my own time and money into working with him to establish a self defence school for young women."

Mr Swithin was beaming.

"A capital idea indeed! I can certainly create the legal documents to establish such a thing as a business, officially. But I sense that you need more from me?"

"We do. The primary thing that we will need is premises for this endeavour – somewhere close to Mr Black's shop, but where we can create multiple discreet accesses to the building, so that young women can reach it safely, but he can still easily go there to teach them at certain times."

"Mmmm, yes, I see – so somewhere that will appear as an ordinary house, but will actually be much more?"

Thorne was beginning to really like this man, whose thinking was so clear and sensible.

"Yes, you have the right of it. I thought that another building on the same side of Sackville Street would be best, with access to the same back lane, which still exists between the rear of the Quadrant buildings, and the rear of the houses along Sackville Street. I have studied the buildings there, and concluded that number twenty-three and number twenty-four – which I believe were originally one house, and were only split to two in the late 1790s – might serve our purpose admirably. There is a sign on them, stating that they are for sale. We would like you to look into it, and discover whether the owner, whoever they may be, still wishes to sell, and if so, what they might want for the two houses. From what I have seen, the houses currently appear to be empty – which may help our cause."

"And if they still wish to sell? What action do you want me to take?"

"Only to inform me, for now – I will need to discuss it with Thomas, once we have whatever information you can find, before we make a final decision."

CHAPTER THREE

Faith stood to one side of the ballroom, and watched the people swirling around her. Beside her, Lady Phoebe Aldwood – the only one of her closest friends from last Season to remain unmarried – watched as well.

"Will any of them ask us to dance? And do we really want to dance with any of them? There seems to be almost no one new this Season, and I can't say that I particularly like the men we already know. But then again, there was so much drama last Season – perhaps we missed being introduced to some worthwhile people?"

Faith rather agreed with Phoebe's somewhat depressing assessment, but she was determined to be positive.

"Surely there will be some new people to meet! I am determined to dance with whoever asks me, just so that I can dance. Now come, let us walk about the room, and see who is here – perhaps someone we know will introduce us to a man we haven't met before."

Phoebe nodded, and they set off, pausing often to speak to ladies of their acquaintance, eventually coming to where a rather large group of people stood, including Marion, and a number of those who had been involved in the events of last year which had restored Faith's brother's honour in the eyes of the *ton*.

Faith was still attempting to get quite straight in her mind the exact relationships of all of these people, who were so closely linked by marriages and friendship, but she was so very glad that they had become part of her brother's, and therefore her, circle of acquaintance. It guaranteed, at least, that there was always someone she could talk to, at any event.

Marion drew them into the circle of people, and Faith quickly looked around, seeing a number of new faces – well, new to her, at least. The Duchess of Windemere, seeing her looking, smiled, and reached out a hand to her.

"Faith, my dear, it's lovely to see you again! We are all trying to make the most of the last few weeks of the Season, aren't we. But I am remiss – have you met everyone here?"

"I haven't, Your Grace."

Faith's eyes had gone back to the man standing not far away from the Duke and Duchess of Blackwater - whose courtship had been fraught with drama last year as well. The man beside them had darkish burnished gold hair and, when he turned a little so that the candlelight caught that hair, there seemed to be deep red highlights in it. He was, she thought, rather stunningly handsome.

"Well, we must remedy that, immediately." The Duchess was a cheerful woman whom Faith admired, so she allowed herself to be tugged forward, and realised that they were going straight towards the man she had noticed a few moments earlier. A man she thought she would be most happy to be introduced to. "If I might interrupt…"

The man turned towards them, as did the Duke and Duchess, who spoke.

"Of course."

The Duchess of Windemere then turned to Faith, indicating the man as she did.

"Lady Faith St. John, if I might introduce Thorne Gardenbrook, Marquess of Wildenhall?"

The man bowed – an elegant, fluid movement, and when he rose, his warm hazel eyes met hers. For a moment, she saw nothing else, and her breath became uneven. Then that moment passed and she spoke.

"I am delighted to meet you, Lord Wildenhall."

She sincerely meant those words.

"And I you, Lady Faith." She hoped that he was as sincere as she was. "Perhaps you might grant me a dance?"

Her heart suddenly became unreliable, its beat a flutter in her chest, and she swallowed. She most definitely did want to dance with him!

"Of a certainty, Lord Wildenhall – I would be glad to. Indeed, I have this next dance free, if that is suitable?"

It was, she realised as she said it, rather unbecomingly forward of her – but she had always been happier with honesty than with being simperingly proper. His eyes had widened, but then, rather than disapproval, his face was transformed by a remarkably dashing looking wicked grin. Her heartbeat stuttered again.

He bowed, more deeply this time, and offered his arm.

"Then we had best proceed, for the orchestra is just starting up for this set."

She placed her hand on the offered arm, and allowed herself to be led away. Behind her, Marion and the Duchess of Windemere met each other's eyes, and smiled, almost conspiratorially.

<<<<O>>>>

Thorne was finding the evening dull, although no one would have known that, to look at him. He was charming, cheerful, and witty in conversation, making remarks about others which edged on improper, but which were saved by the humour in them.

He had mastered the art of seemingly enjoying a Ball long ago, even whilst he cared less and less for them as the years passed. Then, without warning, the conversation in which he was a desultory participant was interrupted, and he turned to find himself face to face with a startlingly lovely young woman. Her eyes were a rich mid blue, her hair was so dark as to be almost black, and her smile was breath-taking.

He barely heard the words as he was introduced, although at least he managed to catch her name. Then reflex and years of training took over and he bowed as she acknowledged the introduction.

"I am delighted to meet you, Lord Wildenhall."

Her eyes met his as she spoke, and it was as if the world around him slowed, as if everything but her had faded away. Eventually, he found the words – but he startled himself, nonetheless.

"And I you, Lady Faith. Perhaps you might grant me a dance?"

He had not intended to ask her to dance – it had simply happened. But now he had done it – it was up to her what happened next.

"Of a certainty, Lord Wildenhall – I would be glad to. Indeed, I have this next dance free, if that is suitable?"

He bowed again, and offered his arm, discovering that he was glad she had said yes – which was most peculiar, for he'd long found most of the young women, even his intelligent sisters' friends, rather uninspiring. And that intrigued him.

"Then we had best proceed, for the orchestra is just starting up for this set."

She placed her hand on his arm, and allowed him to lead her away towards where the dancers were forming up. It was only then that he truly heard the music, and realised that it was a waltz. They took their places, and began to move with the music – movement which was startlingly easy – she danced well, and it was as if they had been designed to fit together. He almost shook his head at his own thoughts, although… it was true that he had never danced with another woman who felt quite like that.

"It is commonly expected that one will converse with one's dance partner, is it not, Lord Wildenhall?"

Her voice jarred him out of those thoughts, and he brought his eyes to hers. He was not used to being chided by young ladies… generally, they sought to charm him, in the hope that he might marry them – a false hope, but one which many of them clung to. Those blue eyes challenged him, and he forgot that they were dancing, forgot everything but her, as their bodies carried on, seemingly without requiring direction. He swallowed – she was just waiting for him, quiet humour in her expression.

"It is, indeed. What shall we speak of? There are many common options – the weather? The most recent scandal, whatever it is? Some inane pastime which one or the other of us indulges in?"

She laughed then, a quiet, lyrical flutter of sound, before answering him.

"I detest speaking of the weather, and I indulge in very few pastimes – I am a sad failure at many ladylike skills, I must admit – which leaves us with scandal. I do not commonly indulge in gossip, for I find it to usually be constructed more of fabrication than of truth, which means that I have no knowledge of whatever is the latest scandal. Do you know of such a thing?"

Thorne was fascinated. She spoke openly, honestly. It was almost like speaking to one of his sisters – and it invoked in him the urge to tease her, as he would have teased one of them. He repressed that urge. He smiled for a moment as they rotated in the dance, contemplating what to say, then it came to him as he remembered a snippet of gossip he'd heard being passed from one man to another, as he had walked by them near the entry to the ballroom.

"Well, I have heard only one piece of scandal recently – and that by accidental eavesdropping, as I passed two gentlemen earlier. So that will have to do. They spoke in hushed tones of having heard that, not long ago, at a Ball, a young lady had, ah… caused rather grievous discomfort to a gentleman, when he had attempted to confer his attentions on her, more forcefully than she wished. They were shocked that a woman would know exactly how to… do that."

He was suddenly uncomfortable. What he had just said was totally inappropriate for when speaking to a Lady. He might have said such things to his sisters... he prayed that she was not offended. But she said nothing, so he turned his gaze to her face again, and was shocked to see that she had gone quite pale.

"Oh my... I can see how gentlemen would find that scandalous..."

There was something in the way that she said it, some hint of emotion which made him suspect that she had no respect for a man who would hold that opinion. Perhaps he should say something else.

"Of course, if that is not a suitable scandal to speak of, we would need to seek another." Her eyes met his again, curious, and that urge to tease overwhelmed him. "Or we could create one together, in some manner..."

She'd gone paler again, and he wondered why this was going so very badly – he never failed at charm! She stiffened a little, and drew herself up, just as the music began to slow.

"I think not, my Lord. But rest assured that, should you attempt anything scandalous, I would have no hesitation in acting as the young Lady they gossiped about did... Although I will admit that I cannot quite imagine you ever being such a cad as that."

A startling amount of relief filled him, as he escorted her back to her friends and the Duchess of Windemere. He did not, he discovered, wish her to think him capable of being a cad.

<<<<O>>>>

After the Ball, Faith fell into bed, telling Meg to rest the following morning herself, and not even think to come near Faith until well after midday. She had arranged with Janie that the following morning, they would go to the dagger maker's shop – it was Janie's half day off, and Faith knew that no one else would rise until early afternoon.

She had known that they would be home very late – most Balls did not end until three of the morning or so, and she was willing to drag herself awake early, so that she might sneak out.

By eight, she had risen, dressed in a plain round gown of a dull brown colour, and wrapped a cloak about her for greater camouflage. It was too warm, it being May, but she would endure. The house was quiet – most of the larger morning chores were long done by the maids and footmen, who were now taking advantage of the quiet time before the family rose. As Faith slipped down the servants' stairs which went from closest to the family suites, down to a passage which let out on the side of the house, close to the garden gate into the lane behind, she prayed that there would be no one about in the lane.

Twice, as she went, she heard footsteps in the servants' passage below, and froze, but whoever it was hurried past, not even glancing towards the stairs, as far as she could tell. She paused at the bottom, peeking out, then sped along the blessedly empty passage and out of the door. From there, it took only moments to slip out through the garden gate.

Faith pulled the cloak around her, its hood up over her head, and walked steadily away towards the end of the lane. She passed no one, and was deeply relieved, as she rounded the corner into the street, to see a cab waiting, with Janie peering out of the window. She was quick to climb in when she reached it, and Janie rapped on the roof, then the cab moved away.

"Did you have any trouble, my Lady?"

Faith shook her head, pushing the hood of the cloak back.

"None at all. I pray that the rest of this expedition goes as smoothly. I am so glad that your cousin is a jarvey – rest assured, I'll pay him handsomely for his trouble."

"Thank you, my Lady."

They lapsed into silence, and it seemed hardly any time at all before they drew up before a respectable looking shop, in a respectable street. The shop windows displayed all manner of gentlemen's accoutrements.

A sign declared it to be 'Bentick and Black, Gentlemen's Outfitters'. Faith turned to Janie.

"Bentick and Black? As in, the Mr Black who is half brother to the Duke of Blackwater?"

"Yes, my Lady – I thought I'd told you?"

"You gave me the name, but I hadn't connected it, in my mind, until now. What if he tells someone that I know about this?"

That thought was most worrying, and a little frisson of fear slid down Faith's spine – was all of this a mistake? Then she pushed that idea aside – it was too late now – she was here, and she was going to proceed with her plan. She pulled the hood back up to cover her hair and shadow her face, then they stepped down from the cab into the quiet street. Faith paused on the doorstep, and glanced around the street – a flicker of motion caught her eye, some houses down on the other side, as if a curtain had been moved – was someone watching them? She shook her head, and followed Janie into the shop – obviously, she was letting her imagination run away with her.

A small bell tinkled as the door closed behind them, and moments later, a man came out through a curtain behind the large counter. Faith caught her breath in shock – he looked, almost exactly, like the Duke of Blackwater. There could be no doubt that they had the same father!

She swallowed, overcoming her surprise, and pushed the cloak back from her face. Janie stepped forward.

"Mr Black, I've brought someone to meet you. I showed her my dagger case, and she wanted to know more."

Faith met his eyes, and saw no judgement or expectation there as he considered her. Then he gave the smallest nod, and spoke.

"Good morning, my Lady – for I believe that to be the right form of address? What do you wish to know?"

Confronted with the question, Faith found that she didn't know where to start.

"I… I want to order a dagger case, similar to Janie's. But I also want to know more about what you are doing, making these things for women, and making them affordable for maids and others with little wealth. It is a remarkably unusual and altruistic thing to do…"

He gave a soft laugh, then, shaking his head a little.

"Almost everything about my life has been unusual – and in the last ten years, I have received, many times, the benefit of unexpected altruism, so it was a logical thing for me to do. The idea came from a maid that my half-brother employed, who had previously worked for a less than well-behaved gentleman. She asked my half-brother if there was a way that she could learn to use a knife, after seeing him practicing his sword work one day. He brought her here, and things grew from that beginning."

"That's very good of you – but surely it must be expensive – the materials to make such things cannot be cheap?"

He smiled as she said that, and Faith found herself even more curious about the man before her.

"They are not – but that doesn't worry me – the inheritance which I received from my father, albeit rather delayed, was more than sufficient to keep me well for the rest of my life. It is not money that limits me, but time. Time to make the women's weapons, and time to teach them how to use them, at least well enough that I am confident that they could assert themselves if threatened. But I have a plan now, and I hope that, soon, I will have that problem solved."

"That is wonderful to hear!"

"Thank you – but now, my Lady, tell me more of the dagger case you wish to order – I'll need your name, but I promise that it will be confidential."

Faith nodded, and they spent the next quarter hour going over the details, before Faith and Janie set off to return to Hungerwood House, before anyone could be aware of their absence.

Barely three hours later, Thomas was still feeling rather shocked by the young Lady's visit. Surely, it proved Lord Wildenhall's point about such self-defence tools being as necessary for young ladies of the *ton* as for their maids. He was, in truth, remarkably pleased, for if they could provide discreet services helping young ladies of the *ton* learn such things, then monies earned from that would greatly assist with helping even more poor women, who could not afford to pay.

He looked up as the bell on the door tinkled, and was glad to see Lord Wildenhall step into the shop.

"My Lord, I am happy to see you – I have some news, with respect to our planned endeavour."

"So do I – I believe that I have identified suitable premises – on this very street! I have asked Mr Swithin to investigate what price the current owners might sell for, and he will contact me as soon as he has information."

"That's wonderful – it can't happen too soon, for this morning, a maid brought the young Lady she serves to see me, because her mistress wanted to obtain a concealed dagger for herself – which certainly seems to prove to me that you are correct about the need for our services, amongst the young ladies of the *ton*. If one has come here, surely there will be many more to follow, if word is passed around..."

CHAPTER FOUR

In less than a week, Thorne and Thomas found themselves the owners of numbers twenty-three and twenty-four, Sackville Street, and faced with a great deal of planning. The houses were in good structural condition, but had not been lived in for some time. The interiors were laid out in a manner which would be useful to them, for, until the mid-1780s, they had been a coffee house, and then a club, which had resulted in number twenty-four, having some larger rooms, which would suit teaching the maids very well.

Thorne began to spend rather a lot of time at Thomas' shop, as they determined everything that must be done to make the houses habitable, and useable for the purpose. And doing all of that would require staff – so hiring some staff became the first need, and those staff had to be people who would support the purpose of their enterprise. They could not imagine any maids disapproving, but footmen, and a housekeeper, might be more of a challenge.

It seemed sensible to begin their search for staff by asking the maids who were already customers – those they had some way of contacting, at least – if they, or others they knew, would be interested in the positions. They did not necessarily expect much response, for it was not a great house, or an otherwise prestigious place to work, but they hoped for at least some interest.

What happened was rather more than that.

Two days after they started to quietly circulate the word of their needs, a steady flow of maids began to appear at the shop, 'just ducking in while out doing errands', to apply for the positions. Many asked about roles as footmen, on behalf of brothers and cousins too. What had begun as a simple process rapidly turned into a challenging exercise in coordination. At least, Thorne thought, as he called in to find Thomas with a list of twenty-five maids and ten footmen that they would need to interview in the next few days, it appeared that they would not have any difficulty at all in staffing the houses.

"Where shall we start?"

Thomas laughed at the question, shaking his head.

"I have been thinking about that. We can't have them all coming here like this – I suspect that the busybodies of the street are taking note of all of these young women coming to my gentlemen's outfitters shop – no doubt it looks most peculiar to them. If we don't want gossip, we must change things, and fast. Which means that we need at least one room of number twenty-three cleaned up enough to interview them in – and that should be a downstairs servants' area room. I'll see if I can find one or two of those who have applied, who are not currently working, and employ them immediately to do that first part of the cleaning."

Thorne nodded, considering the implications.

"That is a good start – but we'll need a housekeeper and a few footmen rapidly too, to clean and set up the whole building. Beyond that, however, I think that we'll need to find someone respectable to live in each house, as our tenants, so that from the street at least, all looks ordinary. Just how we go about finding tenants who will be sympathetic to our cause, and willing to share the accommodations with the school, I am not sure."

"That is a good thought – and it would certainly make our lives easier, as well as providing camouflage for our enterprise. I need to visit Mr Swithin on a business matter anyway, so I'll ask him if he thinks he can help us find suitable tenants."

"An excellent idea! The sooner the better too."

"Can I do any more for you today, Mr Black?"

Mr Swithin waited as Thomas put the papers they had just finished with back into the folio he had brought them in, thinking, as he did, how much had changed since he had first met the fifteen-year-old Thomas, quite some years earlier. He was glad that life had turned out well for the man, after a very challenging start.

"Actually, there is, Mr Swithin. It has to do with the two houses in Sackville Street that Lord Wildenhall and I have recently purchased for our new enterprise."

Mr Swithin met Thomas' eyes, interest obvious in his own.

"Oh? What more can I assist with? I am looking forward to seeing that enterprise succeed."

Thomas gave a short laugh.

"I think that I can assure you of its success. We quietly put the word out through the maids who have already been my customers that we are looking to hire staff for the houses – we've been inundated. And while that is good, it is also a problem. For a start, the houses aren't yet clean enough even to interview people in, and in addition to that, suddenly having many young women coming to my shop is so out of the ordinary that it is certain to attract the attention of other residents in the street. They are likely drawing all of the wrong conclusions! So I've already hired two of the maids who had no employment at this point, and set them to cleaning in number twenty-three, but, after consideration and discussion, Lord Wildenhall and I have realised that the best way to make our enterprise as invisible as possible, would be to have respectable people living in the houses, as tenants. People who would agree to the shared use, and support our aims, as well as helping maintain some secrecy. Perhaps some spinsters with more progressive attitudes, or something like that?"

Mr Swithin nodded.

"Indeed. Gentlemen would not suit, I think – too much chance of them objecting to you teaching women to defend themselves. But spinsters… let me think on it, and see if any possibilities come to mind. Perhaps you should enlist your Aunt to assist, as well – I am sure that she would approve of the enterprise."

Thomas smiled, wondering why he had not thought of that himself, yet.

"I will do that – it's an excellent idea, as we have already had one young Lady of the *ton* come to the shop surreptitiously, enquiring about both weapons and lessons. Where there is interest from one, there will surely be interest from others, and my Aunt could easily facilitate them learning more, without them having to come to the shop. And once we have tenants, the houses will appear completely unexceptional – which is exactly what we want. There should be no touch of scandal associated with it – I've had quite enough of scandal in my life, I don't wish for any more!"

"I quite understand – although you did come out of the last lot of scandal rather well, I think. I will send you a letter once I have anything to report, but there are certain to be some suitable possible tenants out there – likely ladies who are in a position not too dissimilar from the one your Aunt found herself in, before everything was resolved. Such ladies would most likely appreciate the opportunity for a less impoverished life, if, as I assume to be the case, you intend to 'let' the houses to them for a token rent?"

"Yes, that is our intention – in truth, their 'rent' will mostly be paid by the assistance that their presence will provide to our enterprise, and if, in the process, it makes their lives better, than that is all to the good."

"I'd best get on with it, then. I do rather enjoy work that does good in the world, rather than just ensuring that the already wealthy get wealthier."

Mr Swithin stood then, as did Thomas, and they went to the door, where they parted with a smile. As he left, Thomas wondered just what sort of tenants Mr Swithin might find.

Thorne let himself into number twenty-three with the key, and then locked the door behind him. As he stood in the foyer, where elegant fittings attested to the building's past history as a gentleman's club, he imagined what it might look like soon, once the dust was gone, everything polished, and the carpet on the stairs renewed. The answer, he hoped, was beautiful, and perfectly respectable.

He went through to the servants' stairs, then went down to find Annie and Ruth, the maids they had hired to clean, starting in the servants' area belowstairs. He followed the sound of someone humming, until he discovered them in the small parlour close to the front servants' entry door.

"Good afternoon!"

They turned with a squeak of surprise, and Ruth dropped the scrubbing brush she'd been holding.

"Oh! My Lord, you did give me a turn! I didn't hear you coming."

"I'm sorry – I just came past to see how you were getting on with this, and to do a little more looking about myself. I want to see what the access is like from the back garden into the lanes behind, and identify what work we'll need to do out there, first. I locked the front door again after I came in, as I may not come back through here – I might just go out through the back lane and see how easily I can reach the shop from there."

They nodded.

"We'll make sure to check and lock the back door again when we finish on this for today. We're both living here – far better that than staying where we were." Annie shuddered as she said that, and Thorne wondered just what sort of situation they had been in. "We've cleaned part of the kitchen, and the housekeeper's rooms, plus the butler's rooms, so's we've got all that we need down on this floor. That will do until the house is sorted out, if you don't mind?"

"Do whatever works best for you at this point."

They seemed relieved at his words, and turned back to their cleaning as he left them, passing through the partly cleaned kitchen and to the door which led into the small kitchen garden, which was separated by a wall from the main part of the garden.

The wall also cut off some of the sounds of the neighbourhood, but once he went through the gate into the main garden, he could hear the rumble of carts on Vigo Street, and the sounds of people in the area beyond the back fence of the garden. Noting that they'd need to hire a gardener soon too, he walked down the narrow path between rose bushes gone wild, until he reached the back fence, which was lined with mature trees. It was a high fence, obviously intended to guarantee the privacy of the residents – which it would, but perhaps not so much as previously, for above the tree tops, not all that far away, he could see the upper storeys of the buildings of the Quadrant.

He slipped through the gate into the lane, disappointed to find that there was no stable attached to the house – there was a storage shed of sorts, which lined the outside of the fence, but not enough space to keep a horse, or anything else of size. Past that, and he was in the lane itself, which ran along the back of the houses on Sackville street, and also provided access to the livery stables that opened onto Vigo Street, to the scatter of old mews buildings remaining from the houses which had been demolished to make room for the Quadrant, and to the truncated end of Swallow Street. As he walked down the lane, he counted off the houses, and was pleased to see that a narrowed pathway gave access all the way to number thirteen – Thomas' shop.

Close to the exit into Swallow Street, there was a largish stable building – large enough to hold a single carriage, as well as two horses – which appeared unoccupied. It did not seem to be attached to any house, on any of the streets, so he supposed that it was a remnant of the outbuildings of a now demolished house. Cautiously, he pushed open that rather battered door, and stepped in. Dust lifted up as he did, sparkling like motes of gold in a beam of sunlight which came in through a high window. He walked around, and quickly decided that this might be an excellent addition to his property portfolio – assuming that they could discover who owned it.

Smiling, he stepped back out, and carefully pulled the door back until it appeared solidly closed again, then he went back, and turned down the narrow path which led to the back of number thirteen.

Faith found herself, for the first time in a very long time, quite happy to be walking into a ballroom. Her eyes scanned the room, and she told herself that it was simply because she wanted to see who was there – but she knew that she was lying to herself. She was looking for Lord Wildenhall.

Despite the rather dangerous place their conversation had taken them last time she had seen him, she could not forget that waltz, could not forget how it had felt to dance with him. And dangerous but interesting conversation was far better than conversation so bland as to induce ennui. She hoped that he would attend, that they might dance again, that she might discover whether he truly was interesting, or whether she had simply been temporarily failing in her discernment at that previous Ball.

The conversation replayed itself in her mind, again, for the thousandth time, and she shivered slightly. When she had so summarily dealt with Lord Parrington's unwanted advances, she had not, truly, considered the consequences, beyond the fact that he had released her with alacrity. Now, however, the knowledge that the men of the *ton* were whispering about it alarmed her – she had not intended to become the subject of scandal, she would not be so cruel to her brother, after all that he had been through. But perhaps it was too late to prevent it, if rumours already existed.

She pushed that thought away, and continued her observation of the room, even as she walked across it beside Marion. She saw a number of gentlemen she wished to avoid, a number of young ladies she would be happy to converse with – but she did not see Lord Wildenhall. Which made her suddenly irritable. They reached the cluster of people that Marion had been leading her towards, and she allowed herself to be swept up in polite greetings, and then she simply stood there shamelessly eavesdropping on the conversations around her – none of which involved whispers about young ladies applying their knee to a gentleman's private parts, much to her relief.

Faith scanned the room again, and her breath caught – he was here!

She forgot about the conversations around her, and watched Lord Wildenhall, discovering that she wished to know who he spoke to, who he appeared to regard as a friend, and the like. How she could have managed the passage of the previous Season without really noticing him was beyond her – but she had, and now she wished to remedy that inattention.

Perversely, as soon as she had internally declared that intention, her opportunity to do so was stolen by the arrival of a number of gentlemen, all of whom wished to dance with her. She kindly allocated a dance to each of them, but it was a strain, for they were all rather exceedingly dull. As they walked away, appearing happy, Marion spoke softly beside her.

"Why is it that I have the impression that you don't particularly wish to dance with any of them?"

Faith raised an eyebrow in Marion's direction.

"Perhaps because I don't?"

Marion laughed softly.

"My, you have come a long way – I am sure that there was a time when you would have told them that, rather bluntly."

"Only if they had been truly obnoxious. But yes, I have been trying, this Season, to be a little more 'a proper young Lady'. I fear that it really doesn't come naturally to me. I so much prefer honesty and plain conversation to charming surfaces which hide improper intentions, and self-centred pompousness."

"Which makes the *ton* rather a challenge, doesn't it?"

"It does."

Faith contemplated saying more, but as she hesitated, a voice caused her to turn away from Marion.

"Good evening, Lady Faith. Might I hope that you have a dance available?"

Lord Wildenhall bowed as he spoke, his burnished gold hair glinting in the light.

For a moment, Faith could barely breathe. Then her normal sensibility reasserted itself, and she smiled, determined that her voice would be steady, regardless of the fact that her heart was unaccountably racing.

"You most certainly might, Lord Wildenhall." She met his hazel eyes, and impulsively decided to do something she probably shouldn't. "Would the waltz suit you?"

His eyes widened for a moment, and she saw that she had startled him. But he looked pleased, rather than shocked, and a flush of warmth filled her.

"It most definitely would, my Lady." Then he lowered his voice and moved closer, so that no one would overhear. "Perhaps you have, again, the appetite for a discussion of scandal... or the creation of it?"

Faith drew herself up, and gave him a look which she hoped was stern, but she suspected that she failed, for the twinkle of teasing humour in his eyes only grew stronger.

"My Lord, I am a most respectable young Lady – I know nothing of scandal, I am sure." He raised an eyebrow at her, whilst angling his head in Marion's direction. She sighed, pursing her lips a little. "Beyond the scandals which have visited my family previously, of course. But we do not talk about those. They are in the past."

"Then perhaps we shall have to be most creative, in finding something to converse about... But I will leave you for now. Until the waltz is called, my Lady."

He bowed over her hand, and shocked her then by pressing his lips to it momentarily. A rush of heat sped from that spot to engulf her whole body, and stayed with her, even once he had released her hand and walked away.

After that, the evening became a path of tedium, as she danced with other men – whose conversation did not go beyond the weather, the coming hunting season, their estates, or how skilled they were at investing – and the prospect of the waltz was more appealing with every moment that passed.

But when it arrived, something most peculiar happened.

Lord Wildenhall dutifully appeared, offered her his arm, and led her to the floor, where he swept her into his arms with perfect timing, and they began to move. As before it required no thought – they moved perfectly together, and Faith found herself relaxing with a sigh of pleasure. He met her eyes, and grinned at her, as if amused by the sigh.

"I do hope that is a sigh of relief, to be dancing with me, after the rather uninspiring partners you have danced with earlier?"

He really was quite the most extraordinary man! But his directness, albeit wrapped in devastating charm, drew her into what was probably unwise directness of her own.

"Not simply relief, my Lord. Pleasure. For it is a pleasure to dance with you, even if we have not one word of conversation."

Brightness flared in his eyes, and his lips parted in a little intake of surprised breath. Then his smile redoubled, and he licked his lips momentarily, before he spoke again.

"If that is the case, then I will concentrate on... pleasuring... you, my Lady, with my words, or... without."

CHAPTER FIVE

Thomas looked up from the silver note case he was polishing as the tinkle of bells informed him that someone had come into the shop. It was a man – not young, but not all that old either – and, most unusually, the man was accompanied by a woman. They looked somewhat hesitant, yet strangely determined. He wondered why they were there, for they were respectably presented, but did not look to be wealthy enough to afford his wares.

They came to the counter where he stood, and he tucked the notecase and cloth away to give them his full attention.

"How may I help you today?"

The man seemed unsure what to say, and the woman nudged him. He smiled at her quickly, then spoke.

"I am Mr Bellshaw, and this is my wife. We have been informed, by our niece, Janie, for whom you apparently made a… sewing case… that you are looking to employ staff for a house?"

Thomas was slightly startled, for, all but a few young men who might be employed as footmen, every person so far referred to him by the maids who were his customers had been a young woman.

"That is correct. Did Janie tell you anything of my requirements?"

The man and woman looked at each other again for a moment, then it was the woman who answered him.

"Yes. She told us about the 'special features' of that sewing case, and that you wanted to help more young women that way. That you have purchased a property where that will happen, and that anyone who works there must be in sympathy with your aims in helping women protect themselves. I know that you were looking for maids and footmen... but, perchance, do you need a housekeeper, and a butler?"

The implications of that question were immediately obvious to him, and Thomas regarded the people before him again, carefully. They certainly looked like a couple who could be housekeeper and butler in a respectable household, but he wondered why they needed a new position – good housekeepers and butlers tended to stay with one employer for a long time.

"That is a possibility – please tell me why you are enquiring?"

The man spoke this time, and he took his wife's hand in his as he did so.

"We are enquiring because we have just been turned off without a character from our most recent positions. This has occurred because the Lord whom we worked for is a man of most licentious habits, and had taken to accosting my wife more and more frequently, making it harder and harder for her to defend her virtue. When I came upon him two days ago, in his cups, attempting to force himself on Minnie, I am afraid that I lost my composure so far as to strike him. He released her, but then he terminated our employment, and demanded that we leave the house immediately. We gathered all of our possessions as best we could, with the help of the other staff, and sent a message to Janie's mother, who then arranged for her nephew to bring his cab and collect us. We are staying with her, but we cannot impose on her for long. Without her, we would be out on the streets."

They stood there, their faces carefully impassive, but Thomas could see that they expected to be turned away – for in such cases, the servants were often blamed for the employer's failings. He admired their courage in coming to apply, and he felt certain of their sincerity.

He was generally a good judge of character, and he sensed no element of untruth in their words. Best of all, they certainly had reason to support this enterprise.

"So you would have no difficulty with working in an establishment where the underlying purpose, however it appeared on the surface, was to arm young women, and teach them how to defend themselves?"

Some tension left Mr Bellshaw's frame, and the smallest smile appeared.

"No problem whatsoever, Mr Black."

"Then I believe that we should discuss this further. If you would return here at closing time today..."

"Of course! Thank you for your consideration – and for believing that we speak the truth of our situation. Being turned off without a character has put us in a most difficult position."

They spoke for a few moments more, and then left the shop. Thomas immediately drew out pen and paper, and scribed a short letter to Lord Wildenhall, asking if he might have the opportunity to come to the shop at the close of the day, to discuss a 'most interesting development'. He stepped out onto the street, and one of the local urchins immediately scurried up, knowing that there might be a task for him to do, for coin.

With the note on its way, Thomas went back inside to finish polishing the notecase, and to contemplate the fact that everything about this enterprise appeared to be coming together entirely too easily.

Thorne opened the note delivered to him, and then wondered what on earth Mr Black might mean by it. At least this enterprise was proving to be anything but dull!

He had no evening engagement planned for the day, which made it easy to acquiesce to the request, and so, five minutes before the advertised closing time stated on the front door of Bentick and Black, Thorne pushed the door open, and strode in. Standing near the counter, talking to Mr Black, there were two people – a man and a woman, who looked, Thorne thought, somewhat nervous. Mr Black nodded a greeting, stepped past Thorne, and locked the front door, before turning back.

"Lord Wildenhall, this is Mr Alfred Bellshaw, and his wife, Mrs Minnie Bellshaw. Mr and Mrs Bellshaw, Lord Wildenhall is my partner in this enterprise – a fact which is not widely known, and which we would appreciate you keeping to yourselves."

The man bowed, and the woman curtseyed, looking even more nervous now.

"Good day, your Lordship."

"Good day."

Mr Black spoke again, clearly responding to Thorne's curious look.

"Mr and Mrs Bellshaw have applied for the positions of Butler and Housekeeper at number twenty-three and twenty-four. I have just been explaining to them what has been done, and giving them some idea of our plans, with respect to tenants, and the school. They came to me, on recommendation of their niece, who I had made a dagger for, as a result of having been turned off without a character because Mr Bellshaw had the temerity to protect his own wife from the advances of their previous employer."

Thorne clenched his jaw at the words, horrified, yet again, at the behaviour of so many men who were supposed to be gentlemen.

"Mrs Bellshaw, let me, before we speak of anything else, apologise to you for the actions of a man of the aristocracy, who should, by rights, have a far higher standard of behaviour. I can assure you that, if we do decide, after today's discussion, that employing you is the best thing for us, and for you, then you will not ever face that sort of thing whilst in our employ."

They looked utterly shocked by his words, and Mrs Bellshaw stuttered a heartfelt thank you for the assurance.

Mr Black smiled broadly, then went back to the matters at hand.

"Lord Wildenhall, do you have any specific questions?"

"Not at this point – let us proceed to number twenty-three and twenty-four – as I assume you had planned? – and see what questions arise as we show Mr and Mrs Bellshaw the premises."

Mr Black nodded, and, without further words, waved them all through to the back, and out into the lane, locking the door of number thirteen behind him. Once they were walking along the lane, he spoke again.

"I must apologise, Mr and Mrs Bellshaw, for the use of the back lane – we are doing our best to keep this enterprise a matter of some secrecy from the other residents of the street, lest those who might disapprove create unhelpful gossip. We hope that, once we have unexceptionable tenants in the houses, and a full staffing, that none but us, our tenants and staff, and the women who come to us to learn will know of the true purpose of the buildings."

They traversed the lane without passing anyone, and soon went in through the back gate of number twenty-three. Less than an hour later, it had been agreed that Mr and Mrs Bellshaw were to be employed, and that they might move themselves in the following morning. Annie and Ruth were to move into a different room, freeing up the housekeeper's quarters for their proper inhabitant, and from there, they would plan together for the ongoing employment of staff, and cleaning of the buildings.

Leaving their new employees to arrange things amongst themselves, Thorne and Thomas walked back down the lane towards number thirteen.

"I think that I will visit my aunt tomorrow, and raise the idea that you suggested when you looked along here. I am sure that she can make enquiries of others in Swallow Street, and convince them of her sudden need for a mews not too far from her house, of a size to hold a carriage... I suspect that she'll find the whole thing highly entertaining, and she'll certainly support what we are trying to do. Once she discovers who owns the building, we can get Mr Swithin to arrange the purchase."

Thorne looked, again, at the building they spoke of as they passed it.

"It will do very well, I think, as another way for women coming to our school to reach us, relatively unseen."

<<<<O>>>>

Lady Prunella Danby regarded her nephew with an expression of growing delight.

"Thomas! Are you telling me that, now you have been almost accepted by the *ton*, you've immediately set about an endeavour which would thoroughly horrify most of them?"

Thomas laughed and nodded.

"I am indeed. Although perhaps not most of them would disapprove – after all, I am conspiring with Lord Wildenhall to do this. And we have strong indications that many of the young ladies of the *ton* will be most enthusiastic about the idea, if they can manage to slip away to see us, and learn... I suspect that most of the men would disapprove, but the women..."

Prunella looked thoughtful for a moment, then spoke.

"Yes, I see what you mean. Whilst your mother did what she did for love – however misplaced it may have been – there are entirely too many young women who have such things forced upon them. I should imagine that the point of a sharp dagger presented in close proximity to a man's privates might give even some of the most hardened roues pause. But for a young woman to escape her many protectors, safely, to come to a shop, or other establishment, even in a respectable area such as this – that is nigh on impossible, I suspect."

"Indeed. And that is why I have come to seek your assistance, if you will grant it. We have, in this grand plan of ours, a part for you. A part which involves you having become so enmeshed in society that you have developed the need for a carriage and pair, and a place to keep them."

Prunella regarded him with sparkling eyes, quite clearly intrigued.

"I see – and what am I supposed to do with this carriage?"

"Apart from actually be driven about to make your afternoon calls, in your own carriage, rather than in a cab?"

"Yes – for I am quite certain that there is more…"

"There is. But the more is all about the stable building in the old mews area behind the Quadrant, at the end of the now truncated Swallow Street. It is a very short distance from here, being almost directly opposite this house – an ideal location for your convenience, and it even has upstairs quarters where the groom and coachman whom you will employ can live. A groom and coachman who will be men who have sisters – sisters who are maids, who have bought concealed daggers from me in the past."

"I begin to see where this is leading."

"That stable building is perfectly located to provide inconspicuous access to the lane which runs behind Sackville Street – and provides a way to reach both number twenty-three, which will be the school, and number thirteen – my shop."

"And…?"

"Your new enthusiasm for society – which is, I rather think, real, for many have taken to you since you re-joined social activities, especially since your sister reconciled with you – will create a circumstance where young ladies, or older ladies for that matter, will find it desirable to call on you. Calls which will be strategically arranged, as far as timing… so that the young ladies – likely guided by the maids who have accompanied them – can slip through the stables, and then along the lane and into number twenty-three, where they can safely arrange purchases, and be given lessons in using said purchases. The funds raised by young women of the *ton* paying for these services will cover my costs in providing such things to the lower classes and the impoverished for free."

Prunella sipped her tea, and thought. Thomas waited, wondering what insight she might now provide. Eventually, she set the tea cup down with a smile.

"That all sounds like an excellent idea. It will be difficult at first, whilst we discover the first few young ladies of the *ton* who are interested, but as the number grows, we can judiciously make them aware of each other, and then word will spread. And the ones I am first introduced to can introduce me to others. But, in addition, you must make me one of these daggers – and some for the maids we employ in this house, so that all who may see anything of note are involved. First of all, I suppose, we must obtain that building. How do you propose to go about it?"

"I suggest, dear aunt, that we go, once we have finished our tea, and walk across the street. We can ostentatiously examine the building, so that if anyone sees and asks you, you can deliver them the explanation that your social schedule now requires you to have a carriage – and somewhere to keep it. Then, if we are both still happy, I will ask Mr Swithin to discover who owns it, and set about buying it."

"Well… at least part of that won't be necessary – I can tell you who owns it. There are a number of gossips in this street who have lamented to me the diminishment of the street after the building of the quadrant. Their gossip has informed me that it was owned by the gentleman, a Mr Buchanan, who resided in the house between it and the church – and said gentleman has recently died. I am sure that Mr Swithin will be able to discover who his man of business was, and effect a purchase."

"Excellent! Then let us go for our walk, and set about officially 'discovering' that information for ourselves."

Twenty minutes later, they stood in front of the building in question, and began their 'act' of being interested potential buyers.

Faith had asked Janie to arrange for her cousin and his cab to be waiting for her, mid afternoon this time, when her mother and Marion had left to make calls. She had claimed an incipient megrim, and stayed home.

But as soon as they'd left, Faith had changed into a suitably nondescript gown, wrapped a cloak around her, and slipped out of the house, a reticule full of coin tucked into her pockets. Janie had been shocked when Faith had said she would go alone, but had not really argued – after all, Faith was of her employer's family... it was not Janie's place to question her choices.

The previous night's soiree had left her disconcerted, for there had been whispers, again, about 'a young Lady having accosted a gentleman who had been perhaps overenthusiastic in his attentions to her', and whilst she had not been named, she was beginning to think that it was only a matter of time. The gossips of the *ton* were persistent, when they wished to discover something...

Now, she alighted from the cab in Sackville Street, asking him to wait for her, and went to the door of number thirteen. Fortunately, she passed no one on the street, and was quickly able to enter the shop, which was empty. The bells tinkled, and Mr Black came out through the curtain at the back as she pushed the hood of the cloak back from her face.

"Good afternoon Lady Faith. I have your dagger ready for you."

As she stepped closer, he bent to open a drawer which was part of the structure below the counter, and moments later placed a beautiful object on the countertop. Faith gasped – she had not expected anything so ornate. It was beautifully made, and almost a work of art. It was quite clearly a case for sewing implements, made of leather, but scrollwork of silver entwined its way around the leather, giving the case strength, and drawing the eye.

"Mr Black! That is magnificent work!"

He sketched her a bow, and smiled.

"Thank you. Let me show you how the mechanism works."

Faith leant closer to make sure that she could see clearly. He opened the main compartment by moving a piece of the silverwork, and showed her the space where small scissors, needles and thread might be stored. Then, he pointed to a metal piece which appeared just to be the inside of the hinge of the lid.

"If you press on this, whilst also pressing on the spiral of silverwork at the bottom of the outside of the case…" he demonstrated, and the apparent hinge separated from the back of the inside of the case, pulling the lining with it, to reveal a mother of pearl embellished handle which had popped up slightly, "…then the dagger handle will be accessible, and you can slide it out, like this."

The dagger was thin, but the full length of the sewing case, and sharpened on two sides, with a wicked point. It was as beautiful as the case. Faith took it from him, and marvelled at the workmanship again.

"But… with so fine and sharp a point, won't that eventually cut through the cloth and leather?"

He angled the case towards her, pointing deep into it.

"There is a solid metal cup at the bottom, which the point rests in."

"That is very clever!"

Faith produced her reticule, and paid – choosing to pay more than the asking price, for the work impressed her so, and turned to leave, having arranged to come back for a lesson in knife wielding, later, on a day when she might have more time available. But, as she did, the shop door opened with a tinkle of bells, and she found herself face to face with Lord Wildenhall.

CHAPTER SIX

Thorne froze in place, for just a second, then long practice took over. He bowed, as elegantly as one could in a shop doorway.

"Good day to you, Lady Faith."

"Good day, Lord Wildenhall.

She looked, he thought, rather flustered, and her cheeks had flushed quite becomingly. For a woman he had always found to be most self-composed, she appeared quite different now. He raised an eyebrow.

"You surprised me – I do not commonly meet ladies of the *ton* at the gentleman's outfitters."

He wondered what she would say – after all, he had, or hoped that he had, a definite idea about why she might be here – she was usually rather plain spoken and honest about things, but he supposed that this situation might not be one where she felt comfortable being so. For a fleeting moment, an expression of almost panic crossed her features, then she drew herself up, provided him with a bland smile, and spoke.

"Obviously then, other ladies are not as prone to buying gifts for their brothers as I am."

It was an excellent answer.

One only spoilt by the tiny snort of strangled laughter which came from Thomas, where he stood behind the counter. Thorne ignored his mirth.

"Then Lord Hungerwood is a fortunate man to have a sister such as you."

He bowed again, and she acknowledged it with a regal inclination of her head, and swept past him to leave the shop. Which was probably fortunate for her, as he had been sorely tempted to tease, and to raise the inescapable fact that she did not appear to be accompanied by... anyone... as propriety required.

The door shut behind him, and he went towards Thomas.

"I believe that she has your measure, Wildenhall."

Thorne shrugged, not willing to admit that perhaps Thomas was right.

"And was she? Buying a gift for Lord Hungerwood, I mean?"

Thomas assumed a stern expression.

"Now Wildenhall, you know that I can't reveal confidential client information..."

Thorne laughed then, for the irrepressible twinkle in the eye had escaped Thomas' control.

"In other words, no, she wasn't. Might I hope that she was buying a dagger, and that she will be returning for lessons?"

"You can hope... but I will not confirm or deny."

Thorne shook his head, and they moved on to talk of number twenty-three, of the progress made so far, and of Thomas' visit to his aunt.

<<<<O>>>>

Mr Barlow Winthorpe was standing on his doorstep, watching the street. He had nothing else to do, as customers had been scarce.

So he was glaring across at number thirteen, occasionally muttering to himself about 'that baseborn upstart', whilst enjoying the May sunshine. As he watched, two young women – maids, from the look of them – scurried along the street and went into Bentick and Black. Winthorpe frowned. That counted five today – five women going into a gentleman's outfitters in a matter of a few hours. Admittedly, they could simply have been sent on an errand by their employers, but, still, he didn't find that explanation all that likely – surely a man would send his footman or valet for such a task.

What possible purpose could they have, for going to that shop?

Was it, perhaps, a front for something else? The shop definitely made and sold a range of gentlemen's products – but had it, since old Bentick died, begun to deal in other things, in a more clandestine manner?

After all, with a base-born man as its owner, a man who might therefore be likely to be of low moral fibre, who knew what insalubrious transactions could occur there?

He shook his head, disgusted at what the neighbourhood was coming to, and determined to watch even more closely to attempt to discover the truth of what was happening. Perhaps there would be something about it which could turn the tide of customers back his own way. He grimaced, and went back into his shop, thinking hard.

In the house next door, Lady Angela let the curtain drop back into place, her thoughts running along a not too dissimilar path from Winthorpe's, although with quite different ends in mind.

Mr Swithin waited whilst his junior clerk provided the two ladies seated in his office with tea and biscuits. They were older, but not so dreadfully old, well dressed, yet subtly showing evidence of a life lived on the edge of poverty. They were, he thought, representative of what the *ton* did to those who did not fit its expectations.

They sipped the tea, and an expression passed across their faces – a particular expression which he had seen before, on the face of Lady Prunella Danby, not so very long ago. It told him a great deal about just how impoverished these ladies were, without any words needing to be said on the matter. Good tea was expensive.

Only when they put their cups down did he speak.

"Lady Clara, Lady Alarice, I believe that Lady Prunella Danby suggested that you speak to me on this matter?"

They shared a look, before turning their eyes to him and nodding.

"Indeed, she did. She indicated that you were seeking tenants for two houses. Tenants who might be more open in their thinking, perhaps, than most. Tenants who would find the idea of reduced rent in return for… assistance… appealing, where that assistance was about genuinely helping young women, rather than the sort of 'assistance' that men usually offer spinsters of limited means."

Lady Clara had spoken, and there was a slight shake to her voice, as if she feared that they had made a mistake in coming. Mr Swithin hurried to reassure them.

"That is exactly the case, dear ladies. I can absolutely assure you that the assistance required does not involve anything improper, in the sense of gentlemen's advances. It does, however, involve some things, in aid of women's safety, of which many of the *ton* might disapprove."

Lady Alarice waved a hand, and made a little 'pfft!' noise, as if utterly dismissing the disapproval of the *ton*.

"Considering the fact that most of the *ton* disapprove of us anyway - for being spinsters, for preferring each other's company to being married to a man, for wishing to live independently, and for being willing to accept the challenges of limited funds to do so – I do not see that whatever you speak of could make our situation more difficult, unless it involved the carnal expectations of a man."

Her bluntness surprised Mr Swithin – but in a good way.

"Then let me explain the situation. Lady Prunella's nephew, the base-born half-brother of the Duke of Blackwater, owns a gentleman's outfitters shop, from which he purveys all manner of sword canes, knives and the like, as well as the usual note cases, hats, ordinary canes and similar. Of late, he has developed a new business venture, which is rather… unusual. He has been making sewing cases with concealed daggers in them, for maids and women of the streets, and teaching them how to use them in their own defence."

The ladies looked momentarily startled, then they both smiled.

"An excellent idea!"

"I agree – and what started as a charitable act on his part has grown, and now, very discreetly, some young ladies of the *ton* are showing interest as well. Mr Black has brought in a partner in this venture – a gentleman of the *ton*, who has rather unusual attitudes, and they have purchased two adjoining houses, not far from Mr Black's shop and residence, from which to operate this business as a self-defence school for young ladies. But, for reasons that I am sure you understand, those houses need to appear utterly ordinary and respectable. Young ladies coming there to learn will come via the back laneway. This is to minimise gossip, and for the young ladies' own protection. But to achieve this, tenants are required, who are willing to share their place of residence in such a way, and who are in sympathy with the aims of this endeavour. As there are two adjoining houses – which, until twenty years ago, were a single house – what has been proposed is that a door exist between the two houses, and that the front rooms of each look exactly as you would expect for respectable occupied houses, but that the tenants will live primarily in the slightly smaller residence, and the activities of the school will occur mostly in the upper floors and the servants floor of the slightly larger house. To compensate for this rather unusual arrangement, Mr Black proposes to let the houses for a very token rent, and to assist with the provision of appropriate furniture, staff, and the like as well."

The two women had absorbed this with expressions which became more and more interested as he went along.

Lady Alarice was the one who spoke, and Mr Swithin had the impression that she was the outspoken one, with Lady Clara being the more 'proper' and quiet one.

"I do believe that we are very interested in this opportunity, Mr Swithin, if it is all as you say it is. We should like to see these houses, to meet both Mr Black and his partner in the endeavour, and to understand what amount a 'token' rent might actually represent. The rooms we currently live in are not large, and even affording that is difficult, as we each have only a small annuity to support us – so the idea of more spacious premises is very appealing, but we must be sure that we can afford it."

Mr Swithin regarded her for a moment, pleased by the practical approach that she was taking.

"I do not see a problem with any of that, ladies. As far as the rent, the gentlemen are willing to offer you this for £3 a year, in total, for both houses. Your expenses should also be reduced by the fact that the gentlemen will be paying for the furnishings and staff of the houses, and for some basic amenities – like good quality tea – to always be on hand. You will also have access to a carriage, which Mr Black is about to purchase for Lady Prunella's use, and which she has agreed can be made available to the tenants of the houses, as well. I hope that this is well below what you have been paying for small and limited accommodations, and that it will give you the opportunity for a more comfortable life, as well as assisting in the safety of many more young women."

They visibly sagged in what he supposed was relief at the figure he had named, and what it would purchase for them. He wondered then just how miserable their lives had been, in recent years.

"That is a very reasonable figure, Mr Swithin. So – what must we do next to set all of this in motion?"

"Have you been out gambling again?"

Mr George Winthorpe regarded his father with languid arrogance.

"Does it matter if I have?"

Barlow Winthorpe repressed the desire to physically reprimand his son – the boy was too old for that to really be an option any more.

"Of course it matters. You know that business has been dropping off ever since that Duke's by-blow across the street became popular! Where do you think the money comes from? You should be learning all you can about the business, to build it up, not frittering away what it earns."

George yawned.

"I have no real interest in the business, you know that, at least, beyond the fact that it allows you to provide my allowance."

Barlow spluttered, anger filling him.

"You have no interest? After generations of your ancestors building this business up, all you care about is what money you can wring out of it? Would you care more if it was making more money?"

George eyed his father speculatively.

"Perhaps – is it likely to start making more money?"

"It might – if we can work out a way to discredit that bounder across the street, so that the *ton* come back to buying from us. There's something going on over there, mark my words – something not right. All those young women I keep seeing, going into a gentleman's outfitters shop – why would they be there? For all I know, he's setting up a bawdy house or worse!"

For the first time, George actually looked interested.

"That wouldn't be half bad... but no, not in our street – can't bring the tone of the neighbourhood down, can we?"

"No, we can't. But maybe we can put whatever is going on to good use. When you go to those gambling dens, you can whisper in gentlemen's ears about improper goings on, and suggest that they shouldn't buy from such a place."

George looked at his father as if he'd suddenly grown two heads. Never before had his father shown any sign whatsoever of being devious like this.

"But we don't know what's going on…"

"You don't need to. Gossip is all about what people imagine, not about what's actually happening. We just need to start it, and let their fetid imaginations do the work for us."

"Hmmm. I do believe you've the right of it there. This could even be rather entertaining. I'll do it – so long as you keep me in funds."

Barlow groaned, but nodded agreement.

<<<<O>>>>

Faith stared at her brother with a sinking feeling in her stomach. He, oblivious to the effect that his words had just had on her, went on.

"If it wasn't a serious matter, I'd be beyond amused – it's about time that some of these despicable cads faced consequences for their behaviour. They were so utterly horrified – 'someone's arming the maids, even teaching them how to defend themselves – they're spoiling all our fun! First it was some of the society girls learning where to apply a knee, and having the temerity to do it, now, it's housemaids with knives. How's a man supposed to get a little… home entertainment… if the damned chits have knives?'. It made my blood boil hearing them whining to each other about it."

Marion looked as shocked as Faith was – but, Faith knew, for entirely different reasons. On one level, Faith agreed with what Drummond was saying – those men deserved whatever they got – but on another, fear filled her – how long would it be before she was named, in the context of applying a knee? Marion finally managed to find words.

"They truly said that? That's terrible! But… is it true? Is someone helping maids to get knives, and teaching them how to use them?"

"It does sound improbable, doesn't it? But that's what they were saying, in the corners of the card room at last nights Ball. I can't imagine that it was entirely imaginary, with more than one of them saying they'd faced that situation."

Faith swallowed, and tried to look just normally interested in the conversation.

"I, for one, rather like the concept of men, who think that they can just take advantage of a maid in their household, finding themselves at the point of a knife. Perhaps more young women should know how to defend themselves."

Drummond turned to her, his expression curious.

"You sound rather passionate about that idea, Faith – has any gentleman given you cause to feel so?"

She shouldn't have said it!

"Not recently, and never to the extent that I think I would have needed a knife. But there have been one or two who were far from gentlemanly. And a number of girls that I know have had very bad experiences."

Marion looked at her then, obviously remembering their conversation about Lord Parrington, and raised an eyebrow – which Faith ignored. She was not going to tell her brother about having applied her knee to Lord Parrington's private parts. Drummond was frowning.

"In future, please let me know about such things – perhaps I can have a quiet word in the right ears, and get something done about those who choose to behave dishonourably."

"Of course." He nodded, and Marion smiled, but Faith desperately wanted to change the conversation. She would need to think about this later, but right now, anything else would be better to talk about! "But surely, there must have been conversation last night about more pleasant matters? Do men talk of nothing but gambling and their own pleasures?"

Drummond laughed, shaking his head.

"Not a lot – unless you consider hunting, horse racing, or estate management to be pleasant matters?"

Faith shook her head.

"How utterly dull."

CHAPTER SEVEN

Thorne sat with Thomas in the shop, as they discussed all that had been done, and all that was still needed. It seemed impossible that only a few weeks had passed since that morning when Thorne had ridden out, annoyed by the quietness of Elbury house. It was still May, yet his whole world had changed.

That morning had seen the delivery of the chaise and pair that had been purchased for Lady Prunella's use, and their installation in the stable building - the purchase of which had gone smoothly. The groom and coachman they had hired, both brothers of maids who had bought daggers, had looked askance at the state of the building, and immediately set to work to improve it.

The tenants had arrived that morning, with their rather meagre assortment of possessions, and declared themselves, yet again, utterly delighted with the accommodations, and with the enterprise which the houses concealed. Now, as closing time approached for the day, they waited only until Thomas could lock up, so that they could step out via the back lane, and go up to number twenty-three. There was to be a lesson in knife wielding for a small group of maids, for whom this was their half day off, and that would also allow the introduction of the tenants to some of the activities they would see regularly.

"I feel like this enterprise has taken on quite a life of its own, don't you? I could not have imagined something of the scale it has already reached, when we first spoke of it."

Thomas laughed at Thorne's words.

"I can only agree – I had hoped to succeed with this, but the speed with which it has all happened is remarkable – and almost completely due to your involvement. I could not possibly have done all of this, and still kept the shop open, by myself."

"I have been glad of it – it's given me something worthwhile to do with my time, and I can already see how many people's lives it can benefit. It keeps me out of the house, and minimises the number of chances my mother gets to nag me about finding a wife, too – which has to be a very large benefit for me!"

For a moment, Thomas looked sad. Then, as he went to lock the front door and turn over the closed sign, he spoke softly, that sadness echoed in his tone.

"That's one problem I'll never have. But I'm sure that, if my mother had lived, she would have been nagging me about the same things." Thorne nodded, sorry to have made Thomas think of his mother. Although she had been gone many years, it was clear that he still missed her at times. But when Thomas came back to him, all trace of the sadness was gone from his face. "But let us get on up to number twenty-three, and make sure that our students all found their way there through the stables and the back lane."

They went out through the back door, and into the lane, locking things after them, and were soon at the rear entrance of number twenty-three. The new footman had obviously been watching for them, and opened the back door as they reached it, smiling.

"Good afternoon, my Lord, Mr Black."

"Good afternoon, Phipps. Have this afternoon's students arrived?"

"They have. I've shown them up to the lesson room, and served them tea."

"Excellent."

"Also, Lady Clara and Lady Alarice ask whether they, and their lady's maid, may come up to observe the lesson?"

Thomas grinned at Thorne then, pleased.

"Of course they may – please bring them up when they are ready."

The footman bowed, and they went past him, and up the stairs, then turned to the back of the house, where the whole rear area of the next floor up had been opened out into one large room. It held virtually no furniture, beyond some chairs and a sideboard arrayed along one wall. The chairs were occupied by five young women, each drinking tea whilst looking about them with rather wide eyes. They all stood and curtsied when Thomas and Thorne entered the room.

"Do please be at your ease, ladies. Here, you are not maids – here you are students, come to learn how to protect yourselves. You need not curtsey to us here. I trust that you are enjoying your tea?"

They all looked a little shocked, but nodded, then one of them finally got up the courage to speak.

"Yes, sir. Thank you – I've never had tea served to me, like a Lady, before. And it's very good quality tea, too."

"I am glad that you like it. Now please, all sit and finish that tea. Once Lady Clara and Lady Alarice arrive, we will begin. They are very important to this venture – having them living here provides this location with the necessary appearance of complete respectability, so that we may continue to help young women like you. I want to make sure that they know exactly what we do in these lessons. They also provide something approximating chaperonage for you, so that no one can question the situation of young women alone with two men. If they are not here, Mrs Bellshaw, the housekeeper, will attend instead."

The girls sat, and were soon whispering amongst themselves as they waited. Thorne crossed the room, his feet silent on the thick carpets which had been laid down, and looked out of the window.

Below, the garden was neater, already showing evidence of the new care being lavished upon it. He turned back, pulling the drapes closed, leaving the room lit only by the oil lamps which had been hung all around the walls. Not that he thought it possible for anyone to see through the windows, at this height, and from the distance of the other buildings, but it was best to be cautious.

At that moment, there was a tap on the door, and the footman led Lady Clara and Lady Alarice into the room.

"Good afternoon, Lady Clara, Lady Alarice."

Thorne bowed, as did Thomas. The ladies curtsied, their eyes going curiously around the room.

"Good afternoon, Lord Wildenhall, Mr Black."

Thomas indicated the maids, who had all risen again, and now curtsied.

"These are our students for this afternoon. May I present Jane, Annie, Liza, Mary, and Kate."

Lady Alarice smiled.

"We are glad to meet you. We have with us our lady's maid, Linnet, who is also most interested in seeing what you learn."

She waved forward the older, rather worn looking woman who had been waiting behind them, who curtsied to all and sundry, looking rather unsure of what the right protocol might be.

"Please be seated ladies, and we will begin." They did as asked, and one of the maids poured cups of tea for them, then all attention was turned to Thomas. "Each of our students today has obtained a concealed dagger from my shop, to better protect themself. Their reasons for needing to do this vary, but all involve inappropriate advances from men who are larger than they are, and who, in some cases, are their employers, or of their employer's families. The aim of today's lesson is to give them some guidance on the best ways to use those daggers to defend themselves, plus to provide other information on how best to repel the unwanted advances of a gentleman."

One of the girls spoke, her voice tentative.

"Do we do this one at a time? Or will you show us all at once?"

"I will show you all at once, to start, then I will spend some time with each of you individually, to make sure that you have it right."

They nodded, and Thomas began, calling on the footman to assist him as the 'subject', starting with ensuring that they all knew where a gentleman's most sensitive parts might be found, and the quickest way to inflict non-permanent damage in those places. He showed them things that they might do without a knife, and then the best way to quickly bring their knife from its concealed home to being a direct threat in a manner which would cause all but the most insensible of men to stop and back away, or at least rethink what they were doing.

Two hours later, having worked individually with each girl, and also, at their request, with Lady Clara, Lady Alarice, and their maid, he called the lesson to an end. It had been a most satisfactory start to what he hoped would be a very long-lasting enterprise.

<<<<O>>>>

The ballroom was crowded, and the sound of conversation tangled with the sound of the music, creating so much noise that it was near impossible to hear the conversation of a dance partner. Which fact made Faith question her senses, as she came close to Lord Woodtrot again in the pattern of the dance, and he spoke a soft question close to her ear, just before the dance steps moved them apart again.

For a moment there, she thought that he'd said something improbable, and horrifying.

"Is it true, Lady Faith? Did you do what they're saying? To Lord Parrington, that is?"

Surely that wasn't what he'd said....

Lord Woodtrot was one of the fast set, who gambled too much, and dressed with an overexaggerated sense of what they considered style, but, on the whole, he wasn't a bad man. Usually, he was the essence of politeness, and he danced well. Which made it all the more shocking that he might say such a thing. And... if she had heard aright, did that mean that his whole circle of acquaintance knew, and were gossiping about it?

She nearly missed a step at the thought.

Then, the dance brought her back to face him, and he raised an eyebrow, giving her a rather impertinent smile. An ice-cold shiver ran down her spine. Yes, it would seem that he had actually said what she thought she'd heard. The dance turned her away, and then back to him again, and she forced a bland smile.

"I have no idea what you are talking about, Lord Woodtrot. I have danced with Lord Parrington but once this Season, and I am unlikely to do so again. What is it that you are implying?"

At that, as the dance separated them yet again, Lord Woodtrot looked uncomfortable. He also looked as if he did not believe her denial, but knew that there was no possibly polite way in which he could call her a liar. He shrugged, turning around her elegantly.

"Oh nothing, nothing. I don't suppose you'd tell me, even if it was true, would you? Not the sort of thing for a Lady to admit to..."

She kept smiling, praying for the dance to end soon, but glad that he had come to that conclusion without her having to spell it out to him. They said nothing more, until he bid her good evening, having delivered her back to her mother and Marion at the end of the dance. She stood there, then, uncharacteristically silent, just letting the conversation nearby flow over her, as a knot of fear coiled in the pit of her stomach. It was beginning to feel like disaster was inevitable. At some point, the fact that she had done that to Lord Parrington would become public knowledge, and she would suffer at the hands of the gossips and the disapproving dragons of the *ton*.

They would exaggerate everything, and no doubt bring up all of her family's past scandals, again.

The thought of that was enough to bring her to the edge of tears, although she wasn't generally prone to being a watering pot. She was pulled out of her thoughts by a voice beside her. A voice she was glad to hear.

"Good evening, Lady Faith. I do believe that you promised me this next dance."

She turned towards Lord Wildenhall, to find that, whilst his expression was everything that was proper, his eyes sparkled with mischief. It would seem that he knew full well that she had not even seen him before this moment, at this Ball, let alone promised him the next dance. Given that the man who had claimed the next dance was someone she did not really care for at all, she chose to allow herself to be charmed, and took his proffered arm.

"Did I? My memory must be failing me… But I shall forgive you for pointing that out."

Wildenhall laughed softly, and led her towards where the dancers were forming up. Behind her, she heard a sound of annoyance, and knew that the man she had promised the dance to had just discovered his loss. They reached the floor, and only then did she realise that it was a waltz, and at that realisation, her relief that he had saved her from dancing with the other fellow redoubled. After the previous dance, and Lord Woodtrot's impertinent and frightening question, she did not wish to be held close to anyone… except, she found, Lord Wildenhall.

That thought set her heart racing, even though the threat of gossip still hung over her. The music began, and they moved with it, saying nothing for some time, until, eventually, he spoke.

"You're very quiet this evening, Lady Faith – is all well with you?"

She made herself smile, and attempted to force brightness into her expression.

"It is. I have just had a surfeit of… uninspiring… conversation this evening, so I am simply appreciating the pleasure of dancing with you."

"How flattering. Does that mean that you trust my conversation to be more inspiring? Or that we are so in tune that no conversation is necessary?"

He was intentionally flirting with her, again. Yet she was enjoying it, unlike the way she usually felt when men attempted such things. There was just something different about him…

"You may believe whichever you like, my Lord."

He shook his head a little, still regarding her with some concern, which told her that her cheerful façade was not, entirely, convincing. Then, just as she began to relax a little, he destroyed her comfort in an instant.

"And are you pleased with the gift you purchased from Mr Black… for your brother…?"

The words were ordinary, but their impact, after the question from Lord Woodtrot, was intense. The way in which he had hesitated before saying 'for your brother' hinted that, perhaps, he knew what she had really purchased from Mr Black. If that was the case, then it simply made everything worse!

She tensed, and he felt it, for the rhythm of the dance was disrupted for a moment, and he angled his head slightly, his expression even more curious. She swallowed, and licked her lips, her mouth suddenly dry. His eyes followed the movement, and an expression she did not understand crossed his face, fleetingly. She searched for words to answer him – what came was inadequate, yet she had to say something!

"Yes. I am quite pleased – as I am sure my brother will be, at the point when I give it to him."

They danced on, and said nothing more, leaving Faith both relieved and disappointed. How was it that conversations with this man always slipped into dangerous territory, when all she wished for was to enjoy his company?

Something troubled her, Thorne was certain of it. She had looked miserable when he'd first approached her this evening, prompting him to be outrageous and claim that she'd promised him the dance, just so that he could steal her away and hopefully make her feel better. But it seemed that he'd managed to do quite the opposite!

He had thought to ask the question about her purchase teasingly, hoping that she might admit why she had actually gone to the shop, but as soon as he had mentioned it, she had tensed, and her previous unhappy expression had returned, despite her efforts to hide it. It puzzled him – if she had bought something for her brother, surely there was no need for her to be concerned? And if she had, instead, as he suspected, bought herself a concealed dagger, why would she be at such lengths to conceal that fact from him? Surely she didn't think that he would disapprove?

Perhaps she did think that. After all, most men of the *ton* would do so. He did not wish her to think of him as being like them….

Now, as he delivered her back to her mother, he wondered how he might discover the truth of it, how he might ease whatever it was that troubled her. He shook his head – if she did not wish to tell him, it was not his place to pry. But he wanted to…

<<<<O>>>>

"I'm certain that there is something going on. There appears to now be someone living at number twenty-three – and maybe number twenty-four too – but there are too many women going to the servants' doors – after all, they've been there over a week, surely they've employed adequate staff by now? And there are less women going to Bentick and Black, as if the location has just shifted. What if they are setting up a bawdy house?"

George Winthorpe looked at his father, who was pacing about the parlour as he delivered this rambling flow of his thoughts, and decided that his father had become obsessed with the matter.

Still, if he was to extract funds, then he needed to take it at least a little seriously, and start the gamblers wondering too.

"I don't see how we can tell, Father."

"We don't need to be sure, we just need to know that what is happening across the street is peculiar, and to get people gossiping about it. I don't care if it's real, so long as it discredits Bentick and Black with the *ton*."

"I see. Well, I'm intending to go to my favourite hell tonight. If the usual crowd are there, then I'll drop some whispers, as 'drunken observations', and we can see what happens."

"Yes, do that. We need to get our customers back, somehow!"

CHAPTER EIGHT

"Thomas, I'm going to ask you a question I've asked before, and this time I hope you'll give me an answer."

Thomas Black looked at Thorne, his expression curious.

"And why would you think that I'd answer you now, if I didn't answer you the first time?"

Thorne met Thomas's green eyes, and spoke, determined to be truthful, despite the fact that doing so cast him in a perhaps not so flattering light.

"Because I am concerned for Lady Faith St John – concerned enough to pry more than I should. I saw her at a Ball last night, and danced with her. She wasn't herself at all. She seemed worried, or disturbed by something, but when I asked her if all was well, she assured me that it was. So I tried to speak of other things, and I asked if the gift she said she'd bought here, for her brother, had been well received. Instead of giving me a glib answer, she stiffened, and told me she hadn't given it to him yet. And then she was distant for the rest of the evening. So... I want to know what she really bought from you, so that I can hopefully see why mentioning it got such a peculiar response."

Thomas regarded him speculatively, and shook his head a little, almost as if amused.

"I'll tell you, without a problem – I was only teasing you by not doing so when you asked that day. But given that you've a serious concern for the young Lady… She didn't buy anything for her brother – she'd ordered a concealed dagger for herself, after her maid told her about them."

"I knew it! I was sure she wasn't telling me the truth, that day. But, in some ways, this makes me worry more – what threats to her does she expect, that make her want such a dagger?"

Thomas shook his head.

"I've no idea – she gave no indication. But… what makes you care, in this case? Have you a tendre for Lady Faith?"

Thorne's first impulse was to resoundingly deny the very idea – but the words never left his mouth, for the suggestion had immediately made him stop and think – did he hold a tendre for the Lady? It was a startling concept, for he'd never been even slightly truly interested in a young Lady before. But, he realised, he was now. He wasn't sure that it was strong enough to deserve the term tendre, but it was there – an interest stronger than the ordinary, of a certainty.

He would need to consider that in more detail later.

"Ah… not really…"

Thomas laughed then, shaking his head.

"You sound so… certain… of that…"

Lady Angela Heath sipped her tea, relishing the fact that she had actually been invited to this particular little afternoon event. The women in the room were a group of fairly influential people, as far as the gossip circles of the *ton* went, and she had been manoeuvring for almost two years to get herself included in their clique. Today's tea, therefore, had a distinct flavour of satisfaction.

The ladies were chattering about various 'scandals' - but there was nothing particularly worthy of attention – things had been, it seemed, rather dull of late. Lady Angela considered – perhaps this was her chance to ingratiate herself further. One of the other ladies sighed, and, in a mournful voice, proclaimed her displeasure.

"Apart from some of the young men saying ridiculous things about maids fending them off with daggers, or some such unbelievable story, there is simply nothing of note happening at present! Either the gentlemen of the *ton* have stopped having scandalous affairs and the like, or we are failing sadly in detecting them!"

Lady Angela took note of that mention of maids and daggers, wondering if it bore any relation to the things she had seen of late. Probably not, but it was worth remembering. For now, she had more interesting things to tell them.

"Actually..." when Lady Angela spoke, all eyes turned to her, and tea cups were arrested half way to mouths as the room took on an air of anticipation, "...I do believe that I may have detected something quite shocking."

"Do tell us, Lady Angela, at once!"

Lady Angela sipped her tea again, then set her cup down, enjoying being the centre of attention.

"As you might know, ladies, I live on Sackville Street – a street which is the residence to a number of respectable and reputable people. Sadly, over the years, a number of... commercial establishments... have crept in, taking over what were previously residences. But most recently, things have changed – there has been a large increase in the number of people coming to one particular shop – Bentick and Black, a gentleman's outfitters – as it is run by the now well-known, baseborn brother of the Duke of Blackwater. But the increased traffic to that shop has been mainly women!"

This was greeted by gasps.

"Women? Whyever...?"

"I don't know – but I have my suspicions. And, in the last short while, a house which had been empty for some time – number twenty-three – has suddenly been occupied, and now there are an excessive number of people going to its servants' door. Some men, but mainly women – women who appear to be of the servant classes, but not the ones I think to have been employed there."

"That does sound strange…"

"Indeed. It is so strange that I have been able to think of only one possible explanation – that someone is in the process of setting up a bawdy house! On my street of residence! The horror of it!"

Lady Angela staged a very dramatic looking near swoon, and was rapidly provided with a new cup of tea and a cake, as the chatter rose around her. Until her hostess gave an enormous gasp, which caused a sudden silence.

"But… is not number twenty-three and twenty-four Sackville Street the new address of Lady Clara Courtald and Lady Alarice Birchwell? A new address which we had already noted is of a quality which was previously, to our assessment at least, far beyond their means?"

Lady Angela could have cheered at that moment, delighted that the seed she had planted had fallen on such fertile ground. Now she was assured of her place here, and perhaps the disruptions to her peaceful street would be stopped too.

One of the other ladies turned to the hostess, her face filled with delighted, titillated horror.

"You are not suggesting, my dear Lady Pittering, that they have anything to do with it? That they may be… supplementing… their income by such an association, that they might even be… complicit… in the matter?"

At that, the afternoon descended into a chaos of creative speculation.

Lord Parrington stood at the counter in the Winthorpe Emporium examining the silver cigar case he had commissioned. The workmanship was excellent, as he had expected.

Barlow Winthorpe smiled, ingratiatingly.

"Are you happy with it, Lord Parrington?"

"I am. It is beautifully done, as usual. I presume that it is, as we discussed, unique in its decoration?"

"Indeed it is, my Lord. I don't make so many of these any more, but they are always unique. There's less call for them, since so many of the *ton* started dealing with that place across the street, lowering the standards of the area...."

Lord Parrington raised an eyebrow.

"Since it became known that Mr Black was old Blackwater's by-blow, you mean? Half of them only go there to see the subject of a scandal..."

"That's very true, my Lord, I'm sad to say. But what would those who buy there say, if they knew the truth....?"

Lord Parrington paused in his examination of the case in his hands, and met Winthorpe's eyes.

"The truth? What truth is that?"

Winthorpe glanced around, as if checking that no one could overhear, and Lord Parrington leant closer, his expression avid.

"Well, you see, of late, there have been some... peculiar things happening. I'm beginning to think that Bentick and Black is rather more than just a gentleman's outfitters – and that the 'more' is disreputable in the extreme. Lately, there have been a lot of new customers going to that shop – and most of them young women of the lower classes. I don't know quite what to make of it... unless... the place is a front for something shocking..."

Lord Parrington was captivated, Winthorpe could tell.

"Shocking? What sort of shocking?"

"Well… do you think… that maybe it's hiding a bawdy house?"

Lord Parrington stepped back, but his expression held interest, in equal measure to the expected disapproval.

"Do tell me more…"

<<<<<O>>>>>

Faith stood with her brother and Marion, his wife, to one side of the ballroom. Drummond was frowning as he spoke.

"There is the most peculiar gossip going around the card room. Two lots of it, in fact. One is some garbled insinuations about Blackwater's half-brother's shop being a cover for some goings on like a bawdy house, or some other nefarious doings, and the other, just as unbelievable, is a repeat of that nonsense about maids or young women being suddenly armed with daggers, and holding off young men of the *ton* who were 'just trying to have a little fun'. If the latter were true, as I've said before, I'd be happy — men who make unwanted advances deserve to end up at the point of a knife. But I still think it unlikely. It's probably some drunken nightmare that someone has recounted. Still, it's strange — the men usually only gossip about who spent how much on horses at Tattersall's. There was one very odd thing though — at least once, I was sure that I heard your name mentioned, Faith. But it can't have been — someone must have been talking about their faith in their abilities, or the like. It's hard to sort out voices in the tangle of conversation."

Faith discovered that she felt faint, his words having sent an icy chill of fear through her. She was almost certain that he had heard her name mentioned, much though she wished that not to be true. Marion spoke then, oblivious to Faith's stillness beside her.

"That is most strange. And what makes it even stranger is that I've heard some whispers amongst the women about odd goings on at Bentick and Black."

"Oh?"

"Yes – something about too many women going to the shop, and they must be setting up a bawdy house. I can't think where all this could be coming from – I just can't imagine a man less likely to be involved in a bawdy house than Thomas Black!"

Silently, Faith agreed with Marion.

But... what was she to do? Was there any way in which she might affect this? Any way to stop such gossip, to stop it getting to the point where her name became associated with it, in a clear and unequivocal way?

She doubted it – and that left her with fear, and a sick churning in her stomach. But she couldn't just let things go on like this. She had never been one to back away from difficulty, so she would just have to face whatever came. After all, whilst having applied her knee to Lord Parrington's privates wasn't exactly ladylike, it was exactly what he'd deserved, and she certainly didn't regret doing it.

It was time to start thinking about what she would do, if there was very direct gossip about her. Her train of thought was derailed then, when, out of the swirling crowd, Lord Wildenhall suddenly appeared before her. His presence made her smile, even though thoughts of the gossip continued to fill her mind.

"Good evening, Lady Faith, I believe that you promised me this dance?"

She widened her smile at his words, and at the mischief in his eyes.

"Yes, I did – this time..." He laughed softly, and offered her his arm, leading her to the floor. It was a waltz again, and she looked up at him, wondering if he was doing that on purpose – making sure that he danced a waltz with her, whenever possible. "And a waltz again – we seem to be making a habit of this. Are you sure that this isn't another ploy on your part for us to have something scandalous to talk about...?"

She shouldn't have said that! What was she doing? Was she mad? Yet with this man, she always seemed to allow the conversation to go to dangerous places.

He gave her that charming smile, and brought his free hand to his chest for a moment.

"A ploy? How could you think it of me? You already know that if I want something scandalous to talk about, with you, I'll probably just come straight out and say it. You have that… affect… on me."

Those words sent a wash of warmth through her, starting from where her hand rested on his arm. So… she had an… affect… on him? She was rather pleased with that idea, she thought – although she might not tell him – that would be giving all too much away.

The music began, and they started to move. Faith looked up at him, and smiled again.

"Then perhaps we shall have nothing to speak of at all, and can simply enjoy the pleasure of dancing?"

"Ah, but there are things to speak of, scandalous things, things that others whisper about, but do not have the courage to confirm."

The icy touch of fear slipped through her again – did he know? What had he heard?

"And what scandalous things might those be?"

She was a fool to ask, but she couldn't help herself. Somehow, with this man, she felt safe, even though what they spoke of endangered her reputation abominably.

"Whether you've had the need, yet, to use that dagger you bought from Mr Black?"

Faith gasped as he spun her around to the music, her heart pounding. How did he know? She'd told him she was buying a gift for her brother, and at the previous Ball, he'd seemed to have believed her. Why was he asking this now? Still… if anyone was to know, she found that she was more comfortable with it being this man. She, shockingly, trusted him. Still, caution was required.

"What dagger?"

He smiled.

"The one that Mr Black told me you had bought."

She had not thought that Mr Black would do such a thing…

"He told you? I had not thought him one to gossip…"

"He doesn't. I am his partner in a new endeavour – one which aims to make items like that dagger available to more women, and to teach them how to defend themselves in various ways. For now, I'd ask you to keep that confidential – unless you are informing a woman who needs to know how to learn just those things."

There was silence, only the music wrapping around them, as she considered what he had just said. She had not expected any man of the *ton* to know of what Mr Black was doing, and she certainly hadn't expected a man of the *ton* to be involved, to support it. Suddenly, she wanted to know more – just how involved he was, and why, and how that had come about. That he had trusted her with this information also startled her, and pleased her.

The music swept to an end, and thus their private conversation must perforce, also end. She looked up at him then, with a slight smile.

"We must, Lord Wildenhall, speak more of this matter later. We certainly can't do so, here and now."

He returned her smile, and she thought he looked pleased.

"We must indeed. Quite how, I do not yet know, but we must."

He bowed as the music faded away, and then led her back to Marion and Drummond. The thought which was foremost in her mind as he did so, was that Wildenhall might be the thing she had needed – the link to a way to make it possible for more young women of the *ton* to learn how to defend themselves. But would he be willing to help her?

It was well past midnight when the quiet of Sackville Street was shattered by a loud pounding on the door of number twenty-three. Mr Bellshaw, not long in his bed, groaned and rose, pulling a warm robe about himself. He reached the front hall just as Phipps opened the door cautiously.

A young gentleman, obviously of the *ton*, and equally obviously well the worse for drink, wobbled on the doorstep.

"About time! What's service coming to, I ask you." The man shook his head, making himself even more unsteady on his feet, then met Phipps eyes again. "Is this the new bawdy house I've heard whispers about? I could do with the attentions of a woman."

Phipps and Mr Bellshaw exchanged startled glances, before Mr Bellshaw stepped forward.

"It certainly is not, my Lord. Whoever has told you that has his facts wrong." Mr Bellshaw gently put his hands on the young man's shoulders, and turned him around, urging him down the steps to the pavement. "You'd best go seeking your pleasures elsewhere, my Lord."

The man grumbled, but was too foxed to make the effort of objecting. For a moment, he looked surprised to find himself back on the street, but when Mr Bellshaw gave him a gentle push to send him off in the direction of Vigo Street, he went, still muttering to himself.

Mr Bellshaw stepped back into the house, and Phipps locked the door again.

"That, Mr Bellshaw, was strange. Why would he think this was a bawdy house? Why would anyone tell him that?"

"I don't know, but I don't like it, not one bit."

CHAPTER NINE

Shortly before Thomas was due to open the shop the next morning, Phipps came knocking at the back door, presenting a worried face when Thomas opened it.

"Good morning, Mr Black. I'm sorry to disturb you, but something happened last night that we thought you should be aware of."

Thomas frowned, immediately concerned.

"Something happened? Do come in and tell me. Opening the shop can wait a short while."

Phipps sat on the chair in the workroom which Thomas waved him to, and began to speak.

"Last night, after midnight, there was a pounding on the door of number twenty-three. I was on duty, so I went to the door, cautious like, and Mr Bellshaw heard it, and came hurrying up from his bed. When we opened the door, there was a young gentleman there, thoroughly in his cups. He asked us 'Is this the new bawdy house I've heard whispers about?'. We were completely shocked, and we've no idea where he heard that. He was too foxed to tell us either. So we soundly disabused him of that notion, and Mr Bellshaw gently sent him on his way. But we thought you should know, first thing, in case anything else strange like that happens."

Thomas was silent for some minutes, considering what Phipps had said, rather shocked by it. Then he shook his head.

"Thank you for telling me. I don't know that there's anything we can do about it, not right away, but I can ask those I know to listen for any such rumours, so that we can attempt to discover where they are coming from. I do hope that Ladies Clara and Alarice were not too disturbed?"

"No, Mr Black, they weren't troubled. They've both chosen to have their personal chambers in number twenty-four, so's we don't disturb them, and they don't disturb the women who may be coming for lessons."

"That's good – I really want this to go well for them, at all times. We need the respectable appearance that they provide."

Phipps nodded, then stood.

"I'll be off back to number twenty-three then. Good day to you, Mr Black."

Thomas saw him out to the back lane, then went in to open the shop, all the while mulling over the peculiar news that Phipps had just delivered.

<<<<<O>>>>>

"Is it true, Lady Faith?"

Lady Anna Wilmington had sidled up beside her where she stood off to one side of the ballroom, catching her breath between dances. Faith turned startled eyes to her, the now familiar sinking feeling invading the pit of her stomach.

"Is what true, Lady Anna?"

The girl flushed, and her fingers twisted together, but she managed to meet Faith's eyes and answer.

"What they are saying you did to Lord Parrington."

Faith swallowed. What could she say?

She really didn't want to admit to it, for if she did, to the wrong person, the gossip would spread almost instantly, even worse than it was apparently already spreading. And Lady Anna wasn't someone she knew well.

"What are they saying, Lady Anna?"

The girl's flushed face turned a darker shade of pink, and her fingers knotted tighter in front of her.

"That you… that you… applied… your knee… to… an unmentionable place, because… because he was trying to be most improper."

Faith sighed.

"Lady Anna, you know that I am a respectable young Lady – and respectable young ladies don't do such things, and, if they should happen to do so, out of desperation, you also know that they would never admit it. So there is nothing for you to gain by my answering your question – for regardless of what might have happened, I am going to say that I did not do anything like that."

Lady Anna nodded after a moment of consideration.

"I can see how that would be the case. Well…" and here Lady Anna looked even more nervous, "…may I just say that I hope you did, and that if you did, I think you're wonderful. Men like that deserve to be… incapacitated."

And with that, Lady Anna turned and almost ran away across the room, leaving Faith thoroughly startled. That was not, at all, the reaction she had expected.

For the rest of the evening, she was aware of eyes upon her, and of young ladies whispering together, wondering, each time, if they were whispering about her. It was exhausting, and her mood was also a little soured by the fact that Lord Wildenhall was not present, so she could not dance with him, and be distracted by his conversation. But perhaps that was wise, given what they would likely almost speak of. Conversation with him was as dangerous as it was delightful.

She mulled over what Lady Anna had said, and wondered how many of the other young ladies might feel the same. Their mothers would likely disapprove, and their fathers certainly would, but if the girls themselves were of like mind with Lady Anna, then it was even more important that Faith find a way for them to learn how to defend themselves.

Perhaps she should select a few of them whom she thought most sensible and trustworthy, and tell them – or even show them – she could purchase a few concealed daggers from Mr Black, and gift them to a select few of her friends...

Yes, that was definitely worth doing.

By the end of that Ball, she had almost decided who she might gift daggers to and, by the end of the week, after being accosted surreptitiously by young women at multiple soirees, afternoon teas and the like, all with similar questions, she was both elated, and dreadfully worried, for the rate at which the gossip was spreading meant that, sooner rather than later, it was sure to be openly discussed amongst the older women. And that would mean certain damage to her reputation.

<<<<O>>>>

Faith had managed to sneak out of the house again, one afternoon whilst her mother and Marion were out making calls, and Drummond was at his club. It had taken pretending a megrim and, as well as Janie, she'd needed to take Meg, her lady's maid, into her confidence. Meg was excited about the idea, thank goodness, and all too happy to help. Janie had managed to get a message to her cousin, and now, here she was, getting out of his cab in front of Mr Black's shop again.

It worried her that she might be seen, but she had no other way to go about this. She pulled her obviously unnecessary cloak about her, feeling instantly overheated in the late May sunshine, and hurried in through the door of the shop.

It took her eyes a few moments to adjust to the dimmer light after the brightness outside, but when they did, she caught her breath, instantly worried – there was someone standing at the counter with Mr Black! What if it was someone she knew?

Then the man turned, and a flood of relief filled her – it was Lord Wildenhall. She pushed the hood of her cloak back, revealing herself, and he smiled. It was the kind of smile that steals your breath, that makes the person smiling seem three times as attractive as they were a moment before. She felt herself heat, the cloak around her suddenly unbearably warm.

"Good day, Lady Faith. What brings you here today?" It was with relief that she realised that she could tell him, for he already knew that she had purchased a concealed dagger previously. Even as she thought that, he spoke again, seemingly remembering their conversation at that last Ball. "Actually, I suspect that I know. And... we said that we needed to talk more, to complete the conversation which we started while waltzing – what better place to do so than here?"

Well, that had just saved her needing to find a way to raise the matter!

"Indeed. But not here in the middle of the shop – someone might come in, and recognise me. Is there somewhere...?"

Mr Black spoke then, his voice quiet.

"If you'll come this way, I've a small office back here, as well as the workroom..."

Faith nodded and followed him, and Lord Wildenhall, through the curtained doorway behind the counter. There was a short hallway, and then they were shown through another door into an office which was immaculately tidy, with barely enough space for the desk, three chairs, and the shelves and cupboards which appeared to hold files and ledgers.

"This should provide the required privacy."

With that statement, Mr Black stepped back into the hallway, and closed the door, leaving them alone.

Alone.

Just her, and Lord Wildenhall.

It was scandalous, shockingly intimate, and a recipe for ruin should anyone else discover them so.

She took a deep breath, and pushed that thought aside. Lord Wildenhall was an honourable man, of that she was sure. *And…* came the small insidious voice in her mind, *…would it be so bad if he was the one for you to be found with, and forced to marry?*

A shiver ran through her, and she lifted her eyes to find Lord Wildenhall watching her, his hazel eyes full of warmth and mischief.

"So, Lady Faith, this conversation which we need to have… where shall we start?"

An excellent question, which she considered for a moment before replying.

"Perhaps it is best if you tell me more about this enterprise, and how you came to be involved."

He nodded, then waved a hand to the chairs.

"Please, be seated – let us be more comfortable whilst we talk." She settled onto one of the hard upright chairs, and he settled on another, so close that their knees brushed, distracting her, simply by the heat of his nearness. He was seemingly unaware of that effect, thankfully, and simply went on speaking. "Some weeks ago, I came to see Mr Black, to order myself a sword cane, and to inquire about learning to use it effectively, rather than bother my brother-in-law with that request. As I arrived here, a cloaked woman was leaving the shop, carrying a package. I thought that unusual, so I asked Mr Black about it. He chose to honour me with his trust, because my sister is married to his half-brother, and he told me of what he has been doing. I immediately applauded the idea – as a man with seven sisters, who taught each one of them how to apply precisely placed force to dissuade a gentleman from improper advances, I fully appreciated the need for young women – of any station – to learn such things, and to have the tools required to keep themselves safe."

With those words, it was immediately clear why this man, of all men of the *ton*, would support such an enterprise.

"I see. But… why did you become involved yourself?"

He gave a small self-deprecating laugh.

"If I'm to be honest, it was because I was suffering a fit of ennui. Now that all of my sisters are married, I have found myself in a quiet house, with little to do. I liked the concept of what he was trying to do, and it gave me a purpose to fill my days."

Faith preferred honesty, and that admission made her smile.

"Well, despite that being a rather self-focused way of you arriving in this situation, I suspect that a large number of women will be grateful for it, regardless. But tell me, exactly how are things organised? Beyond Mr Black making concealed daggers, and sometimes showing girls how to use them, what are your plans – for I sense that there is far more to this."

He leant back for a moment, as if considering where to start, and that little extra distance between them was something she felt acutely – as both a disappointment, and a relief.

"You are correct, there is more – much more. We have purchased the two houses at number twenty-three and twenty-four of Sackville Street and, whilst we have tenants – two very respectable spinster friends – we are, with their cooperation, actually using the upper floors of number twenty-three as a school of sorts, where the young women – mostly maids to date – who purchase concealed daggers can come and learn how to use those daggers, as well as other ways to defend themselves against unwanted advances. I have hoped, from the beginning, that we might find a way to make that available to young ladies of the *ton*, as well – for I believe that they need such knowledge as much as the maids do. I have been hoping, since the day that I first saw you here, that you might be able to help with that…"

He had leant towards her again as he said that, and, almost as if he was unaware of his actions, on those final words he reached out and took her hands. Warmth filled her, and for a moment, she couldn't think at all.

But what he had said…

"Yes."

"Yes?"

"Yes, I want to help. I have been thinking, ever since our maid Janie first showed me her dagger, and told me about this, that the young women of the *ton* need the chance to learn as well – I just had no idea how to make that possible. I'm still not sure that I do, but we must be able to find a way, if we are both working on it."

Excitement lit his face then, and his fingers tightened on hers.

"Ah, but I believe that I have the beginnings of a way, if you help. Thomas' aunt, Lady Prunella Danby, lives in a house he owns in the next street. And she has agreed to help. We have just acquired, for her use, ostensibly, a stable building. And through that, there is access to the back lane behind Sackville Street. My thinking was that young ladies of the *ton* could call on her, then slip across the street and into the back lane, to then access number twenty-three. But I needed a way for them to be introduced to her."

"And that's where I come in? You introduce me to her, and I introduce selected others to her, and she invites groups of young ladies to tea?" He nodded, and Faith felt a rush of excitement, only part of which resulted from his nearness. "I can certainly do that!"

"I'm sure that you'll like her, too, she has quite the sense of humour."

"Then let us arrange all of this, as soon as possible!"

"Yes!"

He was still holding her hands, and as he spoke, he pulled her forward, and kissed her, a short kiss, full of his exuberance and happiness at having found a way to further this cause, but short though it was, it was as if lightning had struck Faith, and for a moment, she clung to his hands to steady herself as the world spun.

Moments later, he released her and pulled back, looking a little embarrassed.

"I… ah…"

Faith didn't know what to say, and her attempt to speak faded away into the sudden silence. He swallowed, then spoke.

"I do apologise, Lady Faith. I should not have done that, but…"

She cut off his words.

"Do not apologise, for I cannot say that I object, no matter how improper that may be. But we must focus on our purpose here. I came here to order some more daggers, to give to a few close friends. I still need to do that, and you need to make certain of a situation where you can introduce me to Lady Prunella – I believe that she doesn't go about in society all that much?"

She was quivering inside, her mind replaying the moment of that kiss, no matter what she was doing on the outside. Lord Wildenhall looked somewhat uncertain, but then, obviously finding it the easiest path, followed her lead, and turned the conversation back to practicalities.

"Indeed, although she has done so more often than before, since the dramatic events of last Season. I think that if Thomas calls on her, we can make certain that she attends a Ball or soiree soon, where I can introduce you. That way, you can also call on her, then sneak in the back way if you wish to come to this shop, or number twenty-three."

Faith smiled at him, a little shakily.

"Then let us slip back out into the shop and inform Mr Black. It's best that you go first, and then let me know when it's safe to come out."

He left the room, and it felt unaccountably empty as a result. Her lips tingled, and she lifted her fingers to them with a sigh. It was not how she'd imagined her first kiss from a man she actually found interesting might have happened, but it was wonderful, nonetheless.

A short time later, he came back to tell her that the shop was empty, that she could come out. She did, and was soon discussing colours and patterns of concealed daggers in sewing kits for her friends, as if nothing unusual had happened.

Yet it had, and she wasn't, at all, certain what to think about it.

She was still uncertain and thinking more about that than where she was when she stepped out of the shop, seeking her cab, and worrying about how late it had become. As a consequence, she was not as careful as she should have been, and that was brought home to her when a falsely bright voice greeted her.

"Why, Lady Faith St John, is that you? How delightful to see you!"

Faith turned, a twist of fear replacing the other sensations which had been occurring in her stomach, to see Lady Angela Heath, a maid trailing behind her, looking at her with the kind of curiosity with which a cat regards a trapped mouse.

She was doomed. There was no possible way in which gossip would not follow this moment.

CHAPTER TEN

George Winthorpe looked up as his father entered the parlour.

"What are you looking so dark about Father? Has it been another bad business day?"

Barlow scowled.

"It has. Barely any customers at all."

George shook his head.

"What's the point then, if it keeps making less and less money – we might as well just close the shop."

His father regarded him as if he had completely lost his mind.

"And just where do you think the money would come from, for us to live on, if we closed the shop?"

George looked thoughtful.

"I suppose you're right there."

Barlow threw up his hands.

"Of course I'm right! It's all the fault of that baseborn upstart across the street! Him and whatever unsavoury things he's involved in!"

"How can you be sure?"

"We've spoken about this before – I can't be sure of anything, beyond the fact that, since his noble half-brother acknowledged him, half the *ton* have gone to buy from his shop. And now there's all those women going into the place, and something peculiar going on further up the street. I'm sure it's something morally lacking, like a new bawdy house. Regardless of what he's doing, it's all his fault that our centuries old business is beginning to fail! It's unconscionable! And what have you been doing about it, eh? Have you been making comments in the gambling hells, as we discussed?"

George yawned, looking annoyed.

"A few, yes. Nobody seemed very interested."

"Then you'd best try again – and make it sound interesting! After all, the man might as well have stolen your inheritance outright – that's what it amounts to."

Barlow watched as that sank in, and his son's expression went from casually disinterested to concerned, and then angry.

"You're right! How dare he! I'll find a way to make him pay, have no doubt. I'll start tonight. Let's see what a few scandalous and shocking rumours do to his business! Do you know, a few of the fellows have been telling me that they've gone to have a bit of fun with maids in their house, and been met with a knife point – utterly disgraceful! – and they've concluded that someone must be arming the maids. I thought it was their drunken imaginations talking, but now... we can use that – I'll say its Black who's doing it – after all, he's renowned for making personal knives of all kinds."

"That, my boy, is a very clever conceit. You do that, and we'll soon have the men of the *ton* refusing to buy from him. And if they won't buy from him, surely they'll come back to buying from us."

Faith had spent the day thinking about the events of the previous afternoon. It was a tangle of good and bad, from that fleeting kiss to the moment when Lady Angela Heath had recognised her. She was excited about being involved in Mr Black's endeavours to help young women, and had come to the conclusion that she should actually invest in the project – she had some funds, carefully hoarded from her pin money, a habit which she had started well before Drummond had returned and restored their fortunes, and she saw no reason, now, not to invest it in such a worthy cause.

Especially when being involved with that cause would mean that she was in regular contact with Lord Wildenhall...

That was all well and good, however, but what was a far more immediate concern was Lady Angela Heath. Would she be at the Soiree that Faith was to attend that night? Had she already gossiped to those women closest to her? Would Faith walk into a room full of whispers about her own reputation?

Just considering the possibility sent a frisson of fear through her.

Yet there was nothing to be done about it but to attend, and deal with whatever occurred.

Now, some hours later, as she walked into the large parlour of Lady Wells' home, she immediately scanned the room, looking for Lady Angela. Thankfully, there was no sign of her – which did not mean that she might not arrive later, but which was a relief, in the short term.

She followed her mother across the room, and was soon surrounded by ladies deep in conversation. She half listened to it all, thankful that she was hearing no hint of the disturbing rumours she feared. After some time, Lady Wells came over to their group, accompanied by another Lady, whom Faith judged to be somewhat younger than her own mother, but not so very young. She wondered who the woman was.

"Good evening, ladies. Might I introduce you to my sister, Lady Prunella Danby?"

Everyone nodded, and Lady Wells proceeded to provide Lady Prunella with each of their names – no doubt a bewildering list to remember! Faith was delighted, for here, if she had remembered correctly, was Mr Black's aunt, whom Lord Wildenhall had intended to introduce to her. Lady Wells reached Faith in her introductions, and Faith curtsied, smiling at Lady Prunella.

"I am delighted to make your acquaintance, Lady Prunella."

"And I yours."

Lady Prunella regarded Faith with bright and curious eyes. She seemed friendly, and Faith remembered Lord Wildenhall saying that Lady Prunella had an excellent sense of humour. Everyone else was talking amongst themselves again, so Faith decided to take a small risk.

"I recently spoke to your nephew, Lady Prunella, and he suggested that I should make your acquaintance, so this is quite fortuitous. He also told me that you have something of a sense of humour – a thing which I believe to be a pre-requisite for dealing with life amongst the *ton*."

When Faith mentioned Mr Black, Lady Prunella raised an eyebrow.

"I would agree with you on that. I spent so many years not moving amongst society that this last year has been rather... challenging." She paused for a moment and then, after a glance about them, as if to ascertain who might overhear, she continued. "But I confess that I am surprised to hear a young Lady of the *ton* mention speaking with my nephew. Whilst he is accepted, now, he does not commonly move about in society. Might your speaking to him have come about due to his recent new... enterprise?"

Faith smiled broadly then.

"Yes, you have the right of it. But that is not a conversation for tonight, here – perhaps I could call upon you, soon?"

Lady Prunella seemed pleased.

"Of course you must! Then we can speak on whatever subjects please us..."

At that moment, a movement near her caught Faith's attention, and she turned slightly, only to discover Lord Wildenhall approaching.

"Good evening, Lady Faith, Lady Prunella." He bowed, and Faith found herself suddenly short of breath, the memory of that fleeting kiss making heat flood her cheeks. "I can see that you have already been introduced – it seems that I was too tardy to do the honours myself."

Faith curtsied, smiling.

"You were indeed. Lady Wells provided the introduction. I do believe that Lady Prunella and I have taken a liking to each other – I was just arranging to call upon her for tea, at her earliest convenience."

He smiled at her then, another of those smiles which transformed his face, and stole her breath.

"An excellent idea. I am sure that you'll find much to talk about."

<<<<O>>>>

Faith was beginning to wish that the Season had finished, so that she need not go to so many social occasions – she found them increasingly dull, with the exception of the moments that she spent with Lord Wildenhall. That thought seemed to summon him, for he appeared before her, smiling widely – she hadn't even known he was in attendance.

"Good Evening! Might I hope that you have saved a dance for me?"

"I might have, had I known that you were to attend…" His face fell, and she laughed, shaking her head. "But do not despair – by sheer chance, I happen to still have the waltz free…"

"Sheer chance? How fortuitous."

He raised an eyebrow, as if suspecting her of having actually kept it free, in the hope of his attendance. She had – but she wasn't going to admit that, especially not to him.

"Fortuitous indeed that you have arrived here just before the waltz is to be danced, as well."

He gave her a conspiratorial smile then.

"Well… I am sure by now, Lady Faith, that you have become aware of my capacity for careful planning…"

She tilted her head, regarding his innocent expression, and merely raised an eyebrow. He offered her his arm, and she placed her hand on it, knowing that her mother had noted who she was with, and allowed him to lead her around the edge of the room, progressing towards where dancers were forming up, ready for the music to begin.

Eventually, she spoke again, her words soft, and driven by genuine curiosity.

"Careful planning. And what else might you have carefully planned, at this juncture?"

"Now why should you suspect me of having anything else planned?"

"Perhaps because I have the distinct impression that you would die of ennui if you had nothing interesting to do? And because collaborating with Mr Black seems to have led you down rather unexpected paths?"

He nodded.

"It does seem that things around him tend to lead to the unconventional, doesn't it?"

The music began, and he turned her into his arms, making her acutely conscious of his nearness, of the scent of him – a mixture of sandalwood, and other things she couldn't quite identify, which made her think of sunlit forests on summer afternoons. She looked up to find him watching her as they danced, warmth in his eyes – warmth that sent a shiver of pleasure through her.

They said nothing more, simply allowing the dance to move them, each appreciating being in the other's presence. Faith could not help but wonder if he truly found her company as pleasing as she found his. *And if he did?* What did she wish to do about it?

That was a very good question.

And one for which she still had no answer when the music came to an end.

She didn't want it to end, she discovered – she wanted to stay in his arms, in the pleasure of the dance, removed from the need to deal with social conversation at all. But end it did. They twirled to a halt, and he released her, turning and offering his arm.

"Shall we step out onto the terrace, Lady Faith? I do think that it is becoming overly warm in here, don't you?"

She looked up and met his hazel eyes, wondering if this was part of his careful planning too.

"Yes. That would be pleasant, thank you, Lord Wildenhall."

He said nothing then, but simply led her to the terrace doors, and out into the softer warmth of the evening. There were scattered coloured lanterns along the terrace, and down into the gardens just below, but he led her along to the end of the terrace where the light barely reached, away from other people. Only once they had stopped did he say anything.

"Here, we can talk with little chance of being overheard."

"Talk of what?"

"Daggers, lessons, Lady Prunella and more."

He was standing very close to her, facing her – so very close that she felt the soft wind of his breath on her face as he spoke. It was the most intimate sensation she'd ever felt.

"And what do we need to say on those matters?"

"Well... I'd like to say that I am impressed at how cleverly you managed to achieve an introduction to Lady Prunella, and an invitation to tea. When will you call on her?"

"Possibly even tomorrow, unless my mother has something else planned for me. I liked her – and I am very curious to know what she thinks of the entire endeavour."

"That is good. When you call on her, she can show you the back way to Mr Black's shop, and to number twenty-three." Faith had been hoping for exactly that. "Perhaps then you can attend one of the lessons yourself."

Faith felt a surge of excitement at the prospect.

"I hope to. I'd like to ask you a question, if I may."

"Of course."

"You said that you are Mr Black's partner in this enterprise – is anyone else involved?"

He looked somewhat startled at the question, but quickly shook his head.

"No, no one else. Why?"

"Because if you'll both allow it, I'd like to invest in this. I have a substantial amount put aside, and I can't imagine a better thing to put my money into."

She'd shocked him – she knew it. He'd frozen in place, and she wondered if she'd been a fool. Most men didn't think women capable of sensible decisions about business or money, after all. She waited, her heart pounding, her dread growing with every moment.

Then he did the thing she least expected.

He put his hands to her waist, and spun her around with him, bending as he did so to bring his lips to hers. They stopped with a wobble, her back against the stone of the building behind them, and she gave herself to the sensation, melting against him, a quivery pleasure filling her. After a short while she came to her senses enough to tentatively explore returning the kiss, her lips parting softly as his tongue traced their shape.

All too soon, he drew back, keeping his hands on her only long enough to be sure that she was steady. When they fell away, she missed their warmth upon her acutely.

"You, Lady Faith St John, are truly wonderful."

She swallowed, flattered, and somewhat confused.

"And why would you say that?"

"Because you continually surprise me. Because you think so clearly, and you're not afraid to choose to do all manner of things that most young ladies would never consider. I have no objection to your investing – and I am quite certain that Mr Black will have no objection either. But for now, we should go back into the ballroom, lest someone misses our presence."

"Yes, we should."

But in truth, she didn't want to. She would rather that he kissed her again. That thought shocked her, but she would not deny the truth of her feelings on the matter.

As if he could hear her thoughts, he glanced along the empty terrace, seemingly to confirm that no one was about, then bent to her again.

"But before we do, I cannot help but steal the chance to do this again."

The words were a mere breath of sound against her lips, before his mouth met hers in a crushing, incendiary kiss, that, short though it was, left her utterly breathless.

<<<<O>>>>

Thorne had led her back into the ballroom, acutely conscious of the heat of her beside him, of the flush in her cheeks, of the scent she wore, and of his desire to kiss her yet again.

As soon as he had delivered her back to her mother, he had slipped off to the card room, leant against the wall, and watched fools lose money whilst he tried to get his thoughts in order. Thoughts which were full of Lady Faith St John. There was something about her, something which made him reckless. He'd always been careful, he'd never led any young Lady to think that he might want more than dancing and conversation, and now, here he was, having kissed Lady Faith St John on two separate occasions. Which was the very essence of wanting more.

Did he really want more? Had he finally met a woman he might contemplate caring about, truly?

He was beginning to think so. When he'd kissed her, she hadn't pulled away, hadn't behaved as if shocked and horrified, as a young Lady should when accosted in such a manner without warning. Instead, she'd melted against him, had responded to the kiss – tentatively, but with the hint of passion – leaving him breathless and aching.

If he was to be honest with himself, he had to admit that there was no doubt that he wanted more – but did she? And how was he going to uncover the answer to that question?

CHAPTER ELEVEN

Lady Prunella had greeted Faith with some enthusiasm and, once they had taken tea whilst discussing many things, including Lady Prunella's rather acerbic assessment of many of the *ton*, they came to talking about Mr Black, and his endeavours in partnership with Lord Wildenhall.

"I gather, Lady Faith, that you approve of my nephew's latest enterprise?"

"I do, very much so. I discovered what he was doing via one of our housemaids, who showed me the dagger he had made for her, after overhearing me mention the fact that I had rather… summarily… dealt with the unwanted advances of a gentleman."

Lady Prunella raised an eyebrow.

"Summarily? That would be… at the point of a knee?" Faith felt herself flush, but nodded. Lady Prunella smiled widely. "Good for you. I wondered who the whispers were about."

Faith gave a little grimace.

"The rumours are something I wish had not happened. I do not need my reputation ruined, nor whispers of scandal attached to my family. But I do not see what I can do about it."

"Simply be brave, and ignore them. More people will respect you for having protected yourself than will decry your actions. But I suspect you came here today for more than conversation, no matter how delightful it is. Am I correct in assuming that you would like to see my new stable building… and the way through it to the lane behind Sackville Street?"

"You are."

"Then let us take my footman – yours can stay here and take some rest – and go for a walk across the street. If anyone sees us. They will simply think that I am showing off my new acquisition. But once we step through the stable, I can show you where the lane is, and how to get to the rear entry for both Thomas' shop, and number twenty-three, where he is teaching young women how to protect themselves."

"Thank you! I very much want to see all of it!"

In the end, Lady Prunella led her up to number twenty-three, and they both slipped in through the garden gate, then tapped on the kitchen door. Phipps opened it, and bowed.

"Good day to you, Lady Prunella. Neither his Lordship nor Mr Black are here at present, but they did warn me that you might be visiting, and bringing a young Lady with you."

Lady Prunella nodded.

"Good. This is Lady Faith St John, Phipps, and she is keen to see what is being achieved here. She hopes to be able to, selectively, introduce some of her Lady friends of the *ton*, to what is being done here."

Phipps' eyes widened.

"I can show you about, my Lady. Lady Clara and Lady Alarice spend much of their time in number twenty-four, but I am sure that they would wish to meet you as well."

"Then please do show me everything!"

Phipps smiled, and led them through the kitchen, and into the lower hallways.

"Everything down here, my Lady, is very ordinary, so that if anyone comes to call in the normal manner, there is a parlour to meet them in, and all seems like any other respectable house. Upstairs, things are different – upstairs in number twenty-three, everything is dedicated to the teaching of young ladies. Lady Clara and Lady Alarice actually both have their rooms in number twenty-four, although, to the outside world, they each rent one of the houses."

They followed him up the stairs, and into a large room at the back of the house, where the walls between a number of parlours had been opened up, to provide a space big enough to hold many people.

When they stepped into the room, they saw three women – two who were obviously of the upper classes, and one who seemed to be a maid. The two upper class ladies had the look of confirmed spinsters who lived in somewhat straightened circumstances. They were, Faith supposed, not much above forty. The maid was far younger, perhaps in her twenties.

The most unusual thing which Faith immediately noticed was that the three were in deep conversation, with the maid seemingly showing the other two something.

Phipps cleared his throat and rapped on the door frame, causing all three women to startle, and spin towards them.

"Ladies, Lady Prunella has come to visit us, and she's brought Lady Faith St John with her. Lady Faith, this is Lady Clara Courtald and Lady Alarice Birchwell. And Ruth, one of the maids who works here in number twenty-three."

With that, he stepped back and closed the door after himself. There was a moment of silence. Faith suddenly felt utterly out of her depth – no amount of education in the social niceties had prepared her for a situation like this.

Finally, the quiet was broken by Lady Alarice, who stepped forward.

"Lady Faith, welcome to our rather unusual houses. I must assume from the fact that you are here, upstairs, that you know about..." she waved her hand around the room, "...everything?"

"I do – well, the idea of it, anyway. I want to know more."

The ladies smiled broadly.

"That is wonderful! All young ladies should know these things!"

"I was told about this by one of our housemaids – and I've already purchased myself a sewing kit, with a concealed dagger. Now I need to learn how to use it properly. And I am hoping to help young ladies of the *ton* to come here, to learn. But I'm interrupting you..."

Lady Clara waved her hand dismissively.

"Don't concern yourself about that. We live here – well, next door – so we can do this at any time. Ruth was just showing us some of what she's learnt, and, I must say, I wish I had known such things when I first came out."

The maid stepped forward then, with a cautious expression.

"I could show you too, if you like, my Lady? I've been helping Mr Black teach some of the newer girls – he says I've a bit of a talent for it."

Ruth blushed as she said it, but Faith could see that she was pleased to have been praised so.

"Could you? Thank you!

Ruth nodded, and asked to see Faith's knife, so that she understood how it would be removed from its hiding place. Then, with a nod, she set about explaining, and demonstrating, what could be done. It seemed no time at all, but over an hour had passed in fascinating exercise and learning, when Lady Prunella spoke up.

"Lady Faith, I think that we'd best be getting back – your coachman and footman will be wondering where we've got to."

Faith gasped, then nodded.

"You're right. Thank you Ruth. I will definitely arrange to come back soon. And Lady Clara, Lady Alarice, may I call on you, as if it were a normal call for tea?"

"Please do, dear girl – you are just the sort of young Lady the *ton* needs – even if they don't know it."

Faith laughed.

"I don't think that my mother would agree with that – but thank you!"

<<<<O>>>>

Lady Angela looked around Lady Pittering's parlour, judging that all of the ladies who might be expected that afternoon had arrived. She wasn't going to set her delightful little piece of scandal before them until she had the maximum possible audience. One must take full advantage of opportunities after all.

She sipped her tea, and, after a short while, Lady Pittering looked around, smiled, then set her tea cup down.

"Well, ladies, what do we have to relieve our ennui today? Has anything interesting been happening? Or have the *ton* entirely stopped doing anything worth contemplating?"

For a moment, there was silence. Lady Angela let it extend, then, just as it seemed someone else might speak, she pre-empted them.

"I do declare, Sackville Street is becoming a shocking hotbed of scandal!"

Every eye in the room turned to her, and ladies set down teacups, licking their lips in anticipation.

"Oh? What has happened now?"

Lady Pittering was doing her best to sound casual, but Lady Angela could see the intensity of her gaze, and knew that she hung on every word.

"Just a few days ago, as I went for a stroll along the street – one must get some air, you know – when I came to the point where I was about to pass Bentick and Black, the most scandalous thing happened. I could barely believe my eyes!"

Sharply indrawn breaths greeted this pronouncement.

Lady Angela let it hang there, until one of the ladies could stand it no longer.

"What did you see?"

"The door to the shop – the gentleman's outfitter's shop – opened, nearly on top of me, and a young woman came out. A young woman who was entirely alone – not even a maid or a footman with her! – a young woman who I recognised!"

"Alone...?"

"Alone, utterly alone, on a public street!"

A little whisper of delicious horror ran around the room.

"Who... who was it? Who has so disgraced themselves?"

"It was someone who has, until now, always appeared utterly stainless, even when others in her family were touched by scandal. But no more... It was Lady Faith St John!"

There were more gasps, and shocked exclamations.

"Surely not!"

"It most definitely was. I called out to her, and she actually stopped and spoke to me, the brazen hussy. It makes me wonder about all of that, last year, with her brother... What else is that family hiding?"

A chaotic flurry of conversation filled the room, and didn't pause for the next half hour.

<<<<O>>>>

Faith regarded her mother with concern.

"Lady Pittinger's? Mother, has something stolen your wits? Why would we even consider going to Lady Pittinger's musicale? The woman is a gossiping viper of the worst kind."

Her mother had waved Faith's objection away.

"She may be – but she is also very influential. If you are ever to manage to find yourself a husband, you'll need the help of every influential person we can find."

The word 'husband' sent a shiver through Faith. Who could she possibly tolerate enough to marry? They were all dreadful. And she had long discovered that she was far too forthright for the vast majority of the men of the *ton*.

Except, said the small voice in her mind, *for Lord Wildenhall, whose kiss can render me near insensible.*

Lord Wildenhall apparently had no difficulty with her forthright manner... or other things about her. She pushed that thought aside, and returned her attention to her mother.

"If we must. But if her daughter is going to sing, I may, part way through the evening, unaccountably develop a megrim. Some things are simply not bearable."

Her mother shook her head.

"At least try. It is nearing the end of the Season, and I am beginning to despair – you really must find a husband, or by next Season they will all be declaring you an unredeemable spinster."

Faith sighed, knowing that her mother was not being unreasonable.

"I will try, I promise you. But I won't marry a man I can't care for. I'll go and dress for it now for, as you left it so late to tell me, we are short of time."

"I left it so late, because I knew that you would find some way to avoid it, if I gave you any more warning..."

"Pfft!"

Faith turned, and went upstairs, then rang for Meg.

An hour later, she came back down, dressed elegantly, yet in a manner which she was sure Lady Pittinger would regard as suitable for an unmarried woman.

Not long after that, they stepped down from the carriage in front of Lady Pittinger's townhouse. Faith regarded it unhappily. This was not a place she wanted to be. Her mother looked at her sidelong.

"Come now Faith – at least attempt to look pleased to be here. You did promise me..."

Faith pasted a polite smile onto her face, and followed her mother up the steps. She had expected that keeping the polite smile there all evening would be a challenge, but what happened as soon as they stepped into the parlour made it doubly so.

A footman announced them and, in an instant, all conversation in the room ceased, and all eyes turned to Faith. She felt like an insect pinned to a board under that collective gaze. What had happened? For surely, something had, for her entry into the room to cause such a reaction. The silence held, but then Lady Pittinger came rushing over to greet them, her smile even more false than Faith's, and everyone else turned away, and began whispering amongst themselves.

Faith wasn't sure which was worse.

"My dear Lady Hungerwood, Lady Faith, I am so glad that you were able to attend. Do come and we'll get you some refreshment. The musicale will commence shortly – my dear Jemima will be singing first, won't that be lovely?"

"Delightful, I'm sure."

That was, perhaps, Faith thought, the least sincere thing she had ever said. She glanced around the room as Lady Pittinger led them to where footmen where handing out drinks and small pastries, assessing who was present. Most were women she expected, women who were part of Lady Pittinger's gossip circles, and their daughters, but then, across the room, her eyes caught those of a tall woman, and a dreadful sinking feeling filled her.

Lady Angela Heath.

The woman who had seen her leaving Mr Black's shop.

In that instant, as Lady Angela gave her a self-satisfied smile, Faith knew what had happened, knew why the room had gone silent upon her arrival – Lady Angela had, as she had expected, gossiped. Was it worse to be gossiped about for kneeing a man in his unmentionable parts, or for departing a gentleman's outfitters shop entirely unattended?

Faith didn't know, but fear coiled within her as she accepted that she was going to find out, and probably very soon.

<<<<O>>>>

"I'm glad you came today." Thomas patted the object which lay on the counter in front of him. Thorne, who had only just come through the front door of the shop, stepped closer, at first unable to see what lay there – but it became clear as Thomas continued speaking. "I've finished that sword cane you ordered. It's taken far longer than I'd intended, but I think you'll find it's been worth the wait."

He lifted it, and handed it to Thorne, who examined it, then pressed the hidden catch, and slid the sword out of the cane. The blade caught glints of light as it moved, and Thorne held it, feeling for the balance, intrigued by how different it felt from a rapier. This was lighter, and would move faster in his hand. The point looked wickedly sharp.

"That is beautiful. It's a work of art in itself, Thomas."

"I try to make each one unique, and as decorative as it is practical. We'll need to schedule some times for you to practice with it – up at number twenty-three would be best, I think – so that you can really get the measure of it. With enough practice, using it – not just the blade, but the whole process of drawing it as well – will become completely instinctive. Which is what you want if you're set upon, and need it."

"I hope I'll not ever have to worry about being set upon! But you're right, I need to learn it well. I'll make time to come past to start on that in the next few days, if that's possible for you?"

"It is. I've taken to shutting the shop for a couple of hours in each afternoon, to do this sort of thing. Most of my gentlemen customers come in at the end of the day anyway – I assume because the *ton* rise so late – so closing for a few hours earlier makes no difference to the business. And as I've evidence that *you* are capable of rising earlier than most of them, you should be able to manage it."

Thorne laughed.

"Don't tell my mother that – it's remarkably convenient for me if she expects me to sleep later than I do...."

CHAPTER TWELVE

Faith had gone to call on Lady Prunella again. Thankfully, her mother approved wholeheartedly of that friendship, although she was a little curious about what Faith might have in common with the now well-known spinster. Faith had simply said that Lady Prunella was more intelligent than most of the young ladies she knew, and had a far better sense of humour. That explanation had been accepted, for her mother knew full well that Faith was perfectly capable of utterly confusing other young women...

They had been sitting in Lady Prunella's house for some time, sipping tea, and speaking of gossip, and those who passed it on. Faith had, after some edging around the subject, told Prunella about the musicale, and what she suspected had happened.

"You're not going to let them stop you from doing the things that matter to you, are you? I know that gossip is unpleasant, after all, I was ostracised because of it for near twenty years, but you simply cannot let that happen to you. I was a fool to let them control me so. You have the strength of mind to face them and survive, I know it. And, if I'm not mistaken, you've a family who will support you regardless, which is something I didn't have, not back then."

Faith considered her words.

She was right – Faith's family would support her. They might be horrified, but they would close ranks and support her. And they had friends who would do so as well. She could not let Lady Angela and the meddling gossip coterie control her.

"Thank you. You're right – my family will support me. Mother might near faint away from the initial shock of it, but then her anger at someone using gossip against me will take hold, and she will defy them however she can. So… I'll just have to continue, for you're also right that I shouldn't let gossip stop me from doing things I care about. I want to help young women learn to defend themselves. I want to learn more myself. If everything goes terribly wrong, and my reputation is irredeemably ruined, then I will need your advice on life as a spinster too."

Lady Prunella laughed then, shaking her head.

"I don't think you're going to need to worry about that, somehow. There will be a man willing to marry you, without a doubt – you'll more need to worry about whether you might want to marry him – whoever offers for you."

"Hmmm. That's also true. Men have offered for me, and I've refused them all so far. They have been beyond tedious, pompous, selfish, and more. None of them treat me like a person – and I am far more than a dowry."

"Of course you are. But surely there must be at least one who sees you clearly?"

Faith shook her head.

"Not so far."

Unless I count Lord Wildenhall…

That thought sent a shiver through her.

"That is disappointing. But enough of this depressing talk – shall we go up to visit Clara and Alarice? That should distract you nicely, and them, for they seem to have taken a liking to you."

"That sounds to be an excellent idea. I must say, between you and them, I am beginning to think that spinsterhood may not be so bad."

Prunella shook her head.

"They have each other. They have, from what I have seen, always preferred each other's company to that of gentlemen. Whereas I would perhaps have liked to marry. I thought that there would be no hope, but now that society accepts me again, there are a small number of widowers I am coming to like – perhaps, eventually, I may still get that chance. But you – you are young, and I am quite sure that, with the right man, a man who appreciates you for yourself, you would be far happier than as a spinster."

"Perhaps."

Faith left it at that, but she thought about it as they walked across the street, and through the stables into the back lane which led to number twenty-three Sackville Street.

A short while later, as they climbed the stairs in number twenty-three, Faith could hear an interesting range of sounds coming from the large upstairs room – was someone practicing? And if so, what were they learning? The idea made her hurry, for she wanted to learn whatever she could.

So she whisked up the stairs and into the room at some speed – and came to a sudden stop, her eyes wide, her mouth suddenly dry, her heart pounding.

There, in front of her, were two men.

Mr Black, giving direction, and Lord Wildenhall, the blade of a sword cane in his hand, following that direction, going through a series of movements with the sword. That was impressive enough, but what had stolen her breath was the fact that Lord Wildenhall had taken off his coat and waistcoat, leaving him in his shirtsleeves – sleeves which were rolled up, shirt which was open at his neck, his cravat having also been set aside.

He was all golden beauty, his burnished gold hair glinting, the sword reflecting the sunlight which came in through the windows, the light limning his face into a chiselled sculpture.

All thought of anything else departed her mind, and she simply stood there drinking in the sight of him, remembering his lips on hers, and the press of that hard body against hers as he kissed her. She might, she considered, melt away to a puddle on the floor, so much heat had filled her at the sight.

Lady Prunella came to stand beside her, although Faith was barely aware of her presence, and they simply waited until, eventually, Lord Wildenhall spun to a controlled stop, and lowered the point of the sword. Mr Black nodded, obviously affirming that the sword work had been correct, and only then did Lord Wildenhall appear to become conscious that there was anyone else present.

His eyes met Faith's, and she felt colour rise in her cheeks, as if she had been caught doing something she shouldn't. Then he smiled at her, that smile that transformed his face, that made him quite the most handsome man she'd ever seen, and she felt likely to melt all over again. He came to her, after carefully sheathing the sword in its cane, and bowed over her hand, pressing his lips to it for a fleeting moment.

"Good afternoon, Lady Faith. I must beg you to forgive my state of undress, but sword practice is, I have learnt, far more effortful than most other forms of exertion, when correctly carried out."

"I am sure that I can forgive you... under the circumstances..."

He raised an eyebrow, and for a moment, she saw the indolent charm, underlaid with mischief, which he usually presented to the world. Then it slipped away, and what she saw was just him – the mischief was still there, but that false cloak of uncaring indolence was gone, and in its place was the man who cared deeply about helping young women protect themselves.

And seeing that, knowing that he trusted her enough to let her see that, filled her with an entirely different flush of emotion.

Thomas had suggested that Thorne carry his sword cane with him – to get used to using it as a cane, used to having it to hand, and comfortable with that. After all, what use was a sword cane when it sat in a rack at home?

So Thorne was taking his advice – and had immediately discovered that it was wise advice, for to begin with, having a cane felt deuced awkward – he wasn't old and frail, and he wasn't a fop, to add every decoration he could to his person. So he persisted, also watching, when he got the chance, other men who carried canes, studying how they held them, how they used them, and attempting to emulate those who looked stylish in the process.

It was an affectation, and some who knew him raised an eyebrow at the sight, but he ignored them, beginning to enjoy the game of keeping them puzzled, all the while getting used to carrying the thing, to moving it, to having it about him in such a manner that he would be able to use it, should the sword ever be needed. Which he sincerely hoped it wouldn't. Still, it was oddly reassuring to know that he had it, and knew how to use it.

Some days passed, and he spent more time with Thomas, learning, and was pleased to see that a steadily increasing trickle of maids and poorer women were coming to number twenty-three to 'ask about the availability of positions' – which was how they had decided to manage the process, albeit that it put a degree of extra work on Mrs Bellshaw's shoulders. There was no doubt that their hopes for the self defence school for young women were being fulfilled – all, so far, except the part where they hoped to have young ladies of the *ton* come to learn as well.

But there was hope there too, if Lady Faith St John was any indication. The thought of her warmed him through, and he smiled, remembering the look on her face when she'd come upon him practicing. That look had reminded him of the moments he'd kissed her – and made him want to do so again, for it was a look that, if he'd read it aright, made it clear that she wanted to be kissed.

He shook his head – that way lay madness – and marriage! Something that he wasn't ready for yet, no matter what his mother wished to be true. Still... he was not averse to spending time with Lady Faith.

Doing so was certainly more entertaining than spending time amongst the young men of the *ton*. The last few times he'd been to his club, there had been all sorts of gossip discussed – they were worse than the coterie of old women who ruled the gossip at Balls and Soirees! They were nastier too, and more prone to implying outright wrongdoing of the most unsavoury kind.

What he'd heard of late disturbed him, for there had been mentions of a 'possible new bawdy house near Sackville Street', and it brought to his mind the incident that Thomas had told him of, when the man had pounded on the door of number twenty-three in the middle of the night. The last thing they needed was scandal – for the sake of Ladies Clara and Alarice, as well as for Thomas, and for the future of their school.

If scandal became associated with it, before the young ladies of the *ton* had any opportunity to learn, then they would never have that opportunity.

<<<<<O>>>>

George Winthorpe sat in the front parlour on the floor above the Winthorpe Emporium shop, and stared out across the street, thinking. As he'd planned with his father, he'd been adding selected gossip to his conversations with the young men he gambled with. They'd seemed to lap it up, always keen to know about scandals – and to be the first to experience a new bawdy house, if there was one.

But the results were not what he'd hoped for. So far, the men of the *ton* were still buying from Bentick and Black, even when George had implied that Mr Black was morally lacking, and involved in inappropriate doings. Which meant that he needed something more. But what?

The sunlit street below provided no immediate answers, and George studied it as he considered, watching carriages pass by, and people on foot as they traversed the street. A carriage drew up, and man stepped out, going to the door of Bentick and Black. George leant closer to the glass.

He had taken to paying a great deal of attention to exactly who went into that shop. This man, he recognised immediately. It was Lord Wildenhall. Again.

George frowned. Wildenhall seemed to visit Bentick and Black an inordinate number of times – what might he be buying? He rarely came out with anything – at least anything that George could see – yet he came to the shop a number of times a week. The door closed behind Wildenhall, but George was no longer watching – he was staring into the distance, unseeing, thinking.

Could he use this to his advantage? Could he create an even bigger scandal with the gossip? One which would touch upon the men of the *ton* themselves, and create outrage?

He rather thought that he could.

If the *ton* became convinced that Mr Black had been instrumental in leading one of their own astray, into morally dubious activities, then surely they would no longer buy from him?

<<<<<O>>>>>

Thorne rode through Hyde Park, somewhat annoyed with himself, for he had left it later in the day than usual, and the paths were more crowded than he liked. Still, a ride got him out of the house, and was good for him, regardless of having to stop regularly to acknowledge the greetings of others. And it allowed him to think.

What he should be thinking about was how to better spread word of their school for young women – but what he found himself thinking about was Lady Faith St John. Those thoughts were very pleasant, but they would not help move the enterprise forward!

Nonetheless, they filled his mind – when would he see her next? Would it be at a Ball, amongst all that formality? Or at number twenty-three...?

His musing was disturbed when two horses drew up on either side of him, matching pace.

"Have you been holding out on us, Wildenhall? We hear from our… sources… that you've got an… interest… in this new bawdy house people are whispering about. When were you going to tell us?"

Thorne was shocked, and he barely stopped his mouth from dropping open as he turned to meet the eyes of Lord Jasper Harlington.

"What are you prattling on about, Harlington?"

The young man frowned, obviously irritated. His companion, Lord Albert Wardle, spoke then, from Thorne's other side, and Thorne turned to look at him.

"We're not 'prattling on', Wildenhall, we're just interested in knowing the truth of what we hear. Although I must say, you've always projected the image of being oh so well behaved, and to discover that you're up to your neck in something like this – well… that's a bit rich, isn't it?"

Thorne sighed, even as a thread of worry slipped into him.

"Gentlemen, I have no idea what you're talking about."

The two men looked at each other, and their faces darkened a little.

"Well, if you're going to be that way about it… we'll leave you to your ride. But don't expect our business later…"

With that, they rode off, leaving Thorne confused and unsettled. Where were these whispers coming from? And how had his name become attached to them? Surely nothing they'd done had been obvious enough to create scandal like this? Especially as they were teaching girls how to deflect the advances of gentlemen, rather than welcome them…

And what if his family heard such whispers about him? He knew that his father would be horrified. Yet what could he do to stop it? Once whispers began, denials made no difference at all. He rode on, the sun warming him, turning the issue over in his mind. Perhaps he should discuss it with his brother-in-law, Trent.

Trent always knew a lot about what was going on amongst the *ton* – he gathered that knowledge on behalf of Lord Setford, although most people knew nothing about that. But it meant that he might be able to help Thorne discover the source of the rumours – and come up with a way to quash them.

<<<<<O>>>>>

Faith couldn't get the image of Lord Wildenhall, in his shirtsleeves, wielding that sword, out of her mind. It had been beautiful to watch, and had shown her just how muscular he was, under the image of languid cheerfulness which he presented to the *ton*.

She wanted to see that again – almost as much as she wanted him to kiss her again.

But of course, it was unlikely that either might occur. For that would need exactly the right circumstances, and she couldn't see how that might be arranged. Perhaps at a Ball, if there was a terrace….

She shook her head, amused at herself. She had never been one to languish after a man, and she wasn't going to start now – no matter how much she liked this particular man. Instead, she forcibly turned her thoughts to which of her friends amongst the young ladies of the *ton* she might purchase a concealed dagger for, which ones she should introduce to Lady Prunella, or to Ladies Clara and Alarice, as a first step towards arranging for them to visit number twenty-three Sackville Street.

Those visits, if she could arrange them, would change the lives of her friends, she had no doubt. There was nothing quite so satisfying as being able to defend oneself from unwanted advances.

Perhaps the first thing she should do was to invite various people to call on her at Hungerwood House – and include Lady Prunella, Lady Clara, and Lady Alarice in that. Conversation over tea could be the start of deeper friendships, after all...

She went to her escritoire, and drew out a sheet of paper, uncapping her inkwell.

It was time to write a list, and some invitations.

CHAPTER THIRTEEN

"You look shockingly serious, brother dear. It's positively unnatural."

Thorne grinned at his sister and raised an eyebrow.

"Lily, are you implying that I have never been serious?"

"Well… perhaps 'never' is exaggerating, but it has certainly been a vanishingly rare occurrence."

Thorne nodded – he couldn't actually deny that claim, at least as far as what he had allowed his sisters to see of him.

"I have good reason to be serious, which is why I've come to visit you and Trent."

Lily lifted her hand to her heart in an overly affected manner, her eyes filled with a mischief which matched that seen in Thorne's eyes on many occasions.

"You mean to say that you aren't here out of affection for me? I am devastated!"

Thorne laughed, shaking his head.

"I'm not, this time, at least. I have something to discuss with Trent."

His brother-in-law, Trent Weatherton, Marquess of Canterford, lifted his eyes to meet Thorne's.

"You do? What can I do to assist you?"

Thorne glanced around, noting the maid clearing the tea things away.

"Perhaps this would be better discussed in your study."

Trent nodded, and they rose, Lily with them, and left the parlour, going up the stairs to the next floor, where Trent had a sizeable study. Only once they were settled in there, and the door firmly closed behind them, was anything more said.

"So, Wildenhall – what is this about?"

Thorne met Trent's eyes.

"This relates to the… work… that you do for Setford. Perhaps directly, perhaps not." Trent regarded him, obviously curious. "To explain, I'm going to have to reveal something to you – something which I ask you to keep in confidence."

Both Trent and Lily nodded.

"Of course."

"Lately, there has been some peculiar gossip spreading. It started only a few weeks ago, and has steadily increased, to the point where it concerns me, for two reasons. One is that it seems to relate to an… enterprise… I have become involved in, and the second is that, most recently, it has actually included my name."

"That sounds concerning. Do tell me more – what is this enterprise?"

Thorne hesitated for a moment, then went on – he was quite certain that his sister would approve, and almost that sure that Trent would too.

"It began when I visited Mr Black's shop, to buy myself a sword cane – on a whim. As I entered, a young woman was leaving the shop, which I thought strange. So I asked him about it, and he chose to trust me with the truth. He had been creating very clever daggers, concealed in sewing kits, ones which a woman might carry to defend herself, and selling them to maids for a pittance."

"Why?"

"Because he wanted them to have some defence against overly amorous gentlemen. Because of his own mother's life, he was acutely aware of the problem, and decided to do what he could. I was fascinated, and I approved wholeheartedly. Having taught each of my sisters how to apply judicious force to fend off gentlemen, I could easily understand the need." Lily smiled at those words, nodding. "So I asked more. He had decided that he wished to establish a school for self-defence for young women, but he lacked a suitable location, as well as the time to do everything. After some discussion, I decided to become his partner in that endeavour, for I had funds – and time available."

"Why that is wonderful, brother!"

"I'm glad that you think so, Lily. But it has become obvious that others are not so pleased. We expected as much, for we couldn't see the arrogant young men who prey on their servants being happy about it. So we've made sure, as much as possible, to keep it from being obvious. We bought two houses, just along the street from Mr Black's shop, where there is a rear entry off a lane, so that things can be kept mostly away from the public eye. We saw that as especially important, as we hoped to eventually make it accessible to young women of the *ton*, too. But it seems that we were not careful enough – at least that's all I can think of."

"Oh? What has happened?"

"Gossip. Amongst men, more than women. So far. There started to be rumours that someone was setting up a new bawdy house in Sackville Street. Then those rumours started to involve Mr Black. Then one night a man pounded on the door of number twenty-three – one of the houses we bought – disturbing our respectable tenants, who generously allow us to use part of the house for the school, then there began to be whispers about it in card rooms and the like. Then, just these last few days, there have been men sidling up to me and implying that they 'know I'm involved with that new bawdy house'. I don't know why – and I worry about the impact on our family, as well as on the future of this enterprise."

"That does sound strange."

"I can only think that someone in Sackville Street is prone to spending their days observing their neighbours, and managed to notice the larger than ordinary number of young women coming to a Gentlemen's Outfitters shop, or the girls going to number twenty-three, applying to work in the house as maids, and decided that it was all suspicious. But what I don't understand is why they would go to such effort to spread rumours – for it certainly feels like focussed effort."

"I begin to see why you felt the need to tell me."

"Indeed. I thought that Setford might be interested, for this seems out of the standard run of things. And I wanted your opinion on what to do – because I'd like to do something, rather than feel useless and try to fend off strange questions and rumours!"

Trent sat for a moment, staring into the distance, obviously thinking, then brought his gaze back to Thorne.

"I agree that Lord Setford will find this of interest. Any area where things amongst the *ton* happen in a manner out of the ordinary may be a sign of something serious. I'll ask him to set some of his men to watching things around Sackville Street and Swallow Street, as well as generally listening to what they can discover of the gossip, especially around the gaming hells, and amongst the servants who work in the great houses. For now, all you can do, I think, is what you have already been doing – be careful, be aware of things, and try not to give the gossip mongers any material to work with. Not that there is anything wrong with what you, and Mr Black, are trying to do – far from it – but it is the sort of thing that is likely to be regarded as scandalous, and to annoy those men amongst the aristocracy who habitually take advantage where they shouldn't."

Thorne nodded, his expression wry.

"Very true. I became involved in this to relieve my ennui, now that I have no sisters at home to bedevil my days, but I seem to have stepped into something far more… interesting… than I had expected."

That remark brought a snort of laughter from Lily, even as Trent smiled his agreement.

<<<<O>>>>

The room above Bigglesworth's Books was the same as ever, the light from the large windows filling it, and the scent of perfect coffee infusing it with comfort.

Trent settled back in the armchair, and set his cup down.

"So you see, Lord Setford, we have something of a puzzle. One I think it worth setting some men to, at least for a while, to discover if we can find what's at the root of it."

Setford looked contemplative, and Trent waited, sipping his coffee, wondering what he would make of it. The silence stretched, and when Setford spoke, the direction of his words surprised Trent.

"Providing maids with daggers? And teaching them how to use them? How interesting. And useful, I think. As you well know, I have people everywhere – men to watch, and report back when they see something which may be of use to us, protecting the crown, and others. But I've rarely recruited women – they have more difficulty moving about unnoticed, and more difficulty protecting themselves. But this... this changes things, don't you think, m'boy?"

"You.. you think that the maids would make good... spies... if they were armed like this, and felt safer?"

"I do. Which gives me a secondary motivation for doing as you ask, and setting men to discover where this gossip is coming from, and why. It does seem strange that it is so specifically targeted, and has arisen seemingly out of nowhere, with nothing we can see to potentially trigger it beyond the movements of some maids – especially as, to most of the *ton*, servants moving about the streets are nigh on invisible."

"That's true – I hadn't considered that aspect. That makes it rather intriguing, in a way. I hope that your men can turn up some clues, and soon, for, if what Wildenhall says is true, the gossip has been coming faster, and getting nastier, by the day."

Setford nodded.

"We'll discover something, I'm sure. There's always some fool behind this sort of thing, trust me. The big question is – what does whoever is behind it stand to gain?"

<<<<O>>>>

"Faith dear, do try to allow some of these gentlemen to get to know you! How will you ever marry, if you barely talk to them?"

The ballroom was crowded, and oppressively warm, making Faith wish that she could be anywhere else. She gritted her teeth and forced herself to smile reassuringly at her mother.

"I do try Mother, it's just that they are all... uninspiring..."

"Surely at least one of them catches your eye..."

Faith laughed, shaking her head, even as, momentarily, the image of Lord Wildenhall came to her mind.

"Just because a man is handsome enough to catch one's eye doesn't make him intelligent or interesting."

Lady Hungerwood sighed sadly, and seemed about to say something further, when Faith was saved by the appearance of Lord Wildenhall – almost as if her thought of him had summoned him.

"Good evening, Lady Faith. I do believe that this is our dance."

It wasn't, as he'd only just arrived, so hadn't had the chance before to ask it of her, but again, Faith had kept the waltz free... just in case... and she suspected that he knew she had, which brought a blush to her cheeks.

"I do believe that you are correct, Lord Wildenhall."

He offered her his arm, casting a sidelong look at her under a raised eyebrow, his eyes full of mischief.

The evening suddenly felt far more enlivening. She smiled, attempting to look mysterious, and unsure whether she had succeeded. They reached the dance floor, and it was only once they were moving that he spoke again.

"I've had the strangest few days – might I have your opinion on a matter?"

It was not the sort of conversational opening that she had expected. She met his eyes, seeing that he was, apparently, utterly serious.

"Of course, if you wish it."

They rotated, perfectly in tune with each other, and he appeared to consider how best to describe whatever it was. She waited, her curiosity growing.

"I've had a number of gentlemen – mainly from the foppish, racy younger set – sidle up to me in various places, and ask me if the gossip is true, if I'm involved in something scandalous, something happening in Sackville Street. Except that they think it's a bawdy house or the like. I can't, for the life of me, think of why they think that, and why they think it has anything to do with me. Is there... is there anything you've heard in the ladies gossip, which might give any indication?"

Faith felt the familiar icy chill of fear – fear for her reputation, and for her family's reputation. Yet she knew of no link between what Lord Wildenhall had just said, and the gossip which had been swirling around her. Still, the pattern was most familiar – people speaking to her surreptitiously, wanting to know if the gossip was true. Could there be any link between the two? Should she tell him? She swallowed – perhaps she should, at least a little – she trusted him, after all.

"No... I don't think so... although there has been some strange gossip amongst the women as well. Gossip which I fear touches on me."

He raised an eyebrow.

"Indeed? And... are you guilty of whatever scandal they accuse you of?"

She blushed then, concerned.

"Ah… not exactly."

"Not exactly? That sounds rather… uncertain?"

The dance carried them around as she searched for the words to explain. It really was the worst place to be having such a conversation, where others might overhear! Again, it was almost as if he were attuned to her thoughts, for as they came around to the side of the ballroom closest to the terrace doors, he simply spun her away, until they stood at those doors, which he immediately opened, and, without pause, led her through.

When they reached the far end of the terrace, and stood in shadow, far from anyone else, she sighed in relief.

He waited, studying her face.

"Yes, I did, once, apply my knee to an unmentionable portion of a gentleman's anatomy, when he attempted inappropriate things. But somehow, it's as if people think I have done more, as if people think I am involved in something bad. I believe that gossip to that end began after one of my visits to Mr Black's shop, when we… when we…"

"Did this?"

He bent then, and brought his lips to hers, gently, fleetingly, breathtakingly, then stepped back again. Her tongue traced her lips, and she nodded.

"When I left that day – by the front door – I near ran into Lady Angela Heath, just outside, and she hailed me. I expected then that gossip would come of it, for I was alone, with not even a maid. But I did not expect the sort of gossip I am hearing. It seems excessive, and malicious, and I don't know why."

"Then it appears that we have a similar problem. Do you have any idea what we might do about it? For if this continues, it will destroy all chance of making the school successful."

She nodded, her teeth worrying her lip for a moment, considering his words. His eyes settled on her mouth, and his lips parted on a soft exhalation.

Did he want to kiss her again? Did she want him to? She pulled her thoughts away from that, and tried to concentrate on the matter of gossip.

"That is true – but I don't know what we can do, except be even more careful."

He sighed then.

"That was the conclusion I'd come to. But it's deeply disturbing, especially as I've also heard some gossip amongst the men about 'maids getting above themselves' and about 'someone arming the maids'. If the various lots of gossip become intertwined…"

"Then we may well be faced with unavoidable scandal. I hope that we can keep this from spreading, somehow, at least until the Season ends – surely, during summer, the *ton* will forget all about it?"

"We can only continue to listen and observe. But for now, I'd suggest that we forget about it, just for a short while. There are things I would rather do, now that we are alone out here, no matter how highly improper that is. Might I hope that you would not be averse to…"

His wickedly mischievous eyes glinted in the subdued light which reached them from the lanterns, and Faith's heart suddenly pounded in her chest, her breath coming short, and her mouth becoming unaccountably dry. She licked her lips, and he gave the softest of groans. It was intoxicating, the fact that she could have such an effect on him!

A kind of madness took her then, and she lifted her eyes to meet his.

"That hope would be fulfilled. I am certainly not averse to your kisses."

He reached for her then, and pulled her to him, his mouth coming down on hers with an intensity of desire that she had not, until that moment, known existed. She allowed herself to melt into it, to be overwhelmed by his need. She'd had no idea, no idea at all, that a kiss could be so wonderful, so dizzying.

After a short while, he pulled back, releasing her, and she felt cold, even on the warm, near summer night, when deprived of his touch.

He looked away for a moment, as if steadying himself, then spoke softly.

"Thank you. I should not kiss you, yet I do not regret it. But this is not the place. We must go back inside, and be our 'society selves'. I will be so glad when the Season is over, and I can focus on more useful things – like the school. Will you be staying in London for the summer? If you are, then perhaps we can... see each other more often, in Sackville Street?"

Her erratic heartbeat sped up again... was he suggesting...? She hoped so, scandalous as that was.

"Yes, Mother and I will be staying in London. Drummond and Marion will be going to one of our country estates, but Mother prefers London. I will also be glad when the Season is over – Mother still hopes that I will find a man to marry before that time, but I think that unlikely. Still, if I don't, eventually, I will become a spinster, and Mother will be deeply disappointed."

He near gasped, a sharp intake of breath, and she wondered why – what was he thinking?

<<<<O>>>>

Thorne had been feeling buoyed by the previous few minutes, the feel of her lips under his still intense in his mind, but her words cut through that, bringing a sharp pain to his heart. He had known, of course, that she would be expected to marry – all young ladies were – yet he had managed to ignore that idea. But now, now that she put it starkly into words, and he had to contemplate the possibility of her marrying... of her marrying someone other than him... it was like a knife twisting within him.

And the fact that he had such a thought was astounding, terrifying, and utterly confusing. But the thought was there, nonetheless.

When had he come to care for her so much?

CHAPTER FOURTEEN

Lord Setford gave the men in front of him serious attention, knowing that they would only bring something to him if they regarded it as significant.

"Milord, I think there's at least two residents of Sackville Street involved in this gossip. And I don't think they're working with each other at all – not intentionally, anyway. They're neighbours, but they don't talk. The Earl's spinster daughter at number thirty-five spends most of her time, when she's at home, peering around the edge of her drapes, spying on what's going on along the street. But she's above talking to the Winthorpes next door, because they are in trade. And they're the other ones who seem to spend a lot of time looking at what other people are doing – especially the younger one – Mr George Winthorpe."

The second man nodded, and then added his own comments.

"Young Winthorpe's got social aspirations, he has – and a taste for both gambling and gossip. When you've had me watching some of the gambling dens in the past, I've seen him about – hobnobbing with the young fops of the *ton*, trying to pretend that he's the same social status as them. They sneer at him when he's not looking, but they listen to his gossip."

Setford considered that for a few minutes as the men waited.

"Do you have any sense of where his gossip comes from? Is he where it starts? Or does he get it from someone else?"

The man shook his head.

"I can't be sure, but I've not seen him whispering with anyone but those men at the gambling dens – which would suggest that it starts with him – but I don't know why. It's not obvious what he might get out of it, apart from some amusement."

Setford nodded, and stared off into the distance for a minute or two.

"And the woman – what do you think her motivations are?"

"Lady Angela? I don't think she's getting information from anyone else – I think she's just a lonely busybody, watching all of her neighbours, and making things up so that she can be important amongst the gossipmongers of the *ton*. The only people she ever goes and calls on are the biggest gossips of the lot."

"Interesting. Well, keep watching both of them – I want to understand what they hope to gain by spreading the sort of rumours they are. It seems unlikely that there's no relationship between the two lots of gossip – even if they don't seem to ever speak to each other."

<<<<O>>>>

"I think I'm going to need an apprentice. This has all become far larger, and more successful than I ever foresaw."

Thorne leant back in the chair, where they sat in Thomas' small office.

"An apprentice? Where will you find one? Your work isn't exactly just one thing – you work metal, leather, and cloth, depending on what you're creating."

Thomas sighed and pushed a hand through his hair, shaking his head a little.

"I'm not sure. I've started asking the girls who come to learn if they have brothers or cousins who might have both the aptitude and the interest. I'm just hoping that I'll find someone suitable that way."

"That's a good thought – if they come to you that way, at least we'll know they'll approve of what we're doing, rather than being a problem. When we started this, I knew that there would be many who would disapprove, but I never expected the sort of gossip and strangeness we seem to be surrounded by. I still don't know what to make of it, but I'm well and truly worn down by it. It's almost like someone wants to create a big scandal before the Season ends, before most of the *ton* leave London for the summer, but I can't imagine why they'd want that – and why target your shop, in this street?"

Thomas shook his head too.

"I can't imagine why, either. Although... a few of the girls have told me, when they've come for lessons, that they've had cause to use their daggers, as deterrents, at least, and then later they've heard the young Lords they've fended off talking with other young men, and complaining about 'maids getting above themselves' and the like. I suppose that sort of reaction was inevitable too. At least, so far, only a small number of them have been turned off without a reference as a result of defending themselves."

"Yes – we don't want them all losing their positions as a result of what we teach them. Hopefully the young men will get more cautious about trying to take advantage of their servants, and all of this will settle down. Although... Some of the set who spend most of their time gambling, or chasing after women they shouldn't, are the kind of men who don't necessarily learn easily..."

"Then we'll just have to keep paying attention to what's being said, won't we?"

Thorne sighed heavily.

"Yes – I don't see what else we can do."

Trent sipped his coffee, watching Setford's expression.

The man's piercing grey eyes were focussed on the rooftops of London, seen through the window, and Trent knew that he was thinking, analysing things carefully before saying anything. The silence extended, until, many minutes later, Setford brought his gaze back to meet Trent's eyes.

"I still don't know why this targeted gossip is happening. My men have narrowed it down to two people we suspect of initiating most, if not all, of it – but we still don't have any good leads on the matter of just why they are doing it. And the two don't seem to be collaborating, even though the gossip is closing in on the same topics and people."

"That's disturbing – and very strange."

"Indeed, m'boy, it is. What I have become certain of – not with any proof, at this point, mind – is that the gossip is intended to create a stir amongst the *ton*, to create a perceived scandal, whether there is actually one or not. I don't know what that might achieve for these people – yet. So I've decided to post men close about the various houses where large Balls and Soirees are held, just to watch, in case something unexpected comes of it. I'd like you to keep your ears open on the matter too – let's see if between your inside advantage, and my men's 'invisibility' as servants and guards, you can discover what's really going on. I'll still keep men watching Sackville Street, and the gaming hells, of course, but we need to find some logic in this, some link between it all."

"I will, as I always do – but I'll pay extra attention, and I'll get Lily to see what she can garner from the women's gossip."

"Excellent! We can only hope that soon, we'll discover the key to it all."

George Winthorpe was feeling aggrieved.

That day, he'd been walking down Sackville Street, after a short visit to the public house on the Vigo Street corner, when he'd nearly collided with a young woman who was coming out of number twenty-three, a maid following her. He'd recognised her immediately – he'd seen her in the street a number of times of late, and some of those times alone, and some of those times going into Bentick and Black, where a Lady shouldn't be.

He'd discovered, with some careful enquiries after the first few times he'd seen her, that her name was Lady Faith St John. So when he'd nearly collided with her, he'd seen it as providence, and greeted her politely. She'd turned up her nose at him, muttering some hoity-toity nonsense about them not having been introduced, and then she'd hurried away.

She obviously thought he was beneath her, the arrogant piece – and her having behaved scandalously, being out by herself before, and the like! If she was going in and out of Bentick and Black by herself, and now number twenty-three, that he was almost sure was a front for a new bawdy house, then she was a long way from the morally upright proper piece she pretended to be, now wasn't she?

It had rankled at the time, and it still did, as he slid onto a stool at the bar in one of his favourite hells, and accepted his usual brandy from the barman. He looked around, sure that his 'friends' would arrive soon, so that he could, before playing a few hands, wind them up with gossip again, and see what they had to complain about. Of late, what they'd complained about had usually been maids rejecting their advances, sometimes at the point of a knife. Ludicrous – but they were all fired up about it.

It struck him then that, perhaps, he could use both the 'maids with knives' gossip, and Lady Faith's high stickler ways against her, and boost the value of his gossip for turning the *ton* away from Bentick and Black. That would be satisfying – furthering the campaign to turn the *ton* away from buying from Black, while at the same time getting a little revenge on the woman for acting as if he was beneath her.

He smiled then, sipping his drink, and considered exactly what he would say, and to who – which of the men he saw most often, here, was more likely to fly into a rage about uppity women?

Half a glass of brandy later, he'd come to a conclusion, and was most pleased when he saw three men coming towards him, including Lord Charles Heath – the one George had decided would be easiest to agitate.

"Evening George – not playing yet?"

George shook his head.

"Thought I'd drink a bit first, and wait for congenial company – and here you are!" They laughed at his words, and quickly ordered drinks. He waited until they'd settled onto seats, then asked a question sure to set things rolling. "So, do tell me – what's been happening the last few days – are there new dramas in your lives?"

"New dramas? More like the same ones! Damned uppity women – none of the maids in the house are being… cooperative… any more, and Father has forbidden me from turning them off for it! Of course, I haven't told him what they've done – too damned embarrassing – but I've told him they're getting above themselves. He just says that he and Mother are happy with them, and it's not my place to deal with the servants like that! How's a man supposed to get a bit of relief if all the maids have knives, I ask you?"

George assumed a commiserating expression.

"It's shocking, I agree – what's the world coming to, I ask you? Still, it may get easier – I keep seeing things going on in Sackville Street, and I'm sure someone's setting up a bawdy house, like I've said before – I know it's got something to do with Bentick and Black – and what would you expect, with him base-born and all? – and I think it's also got something to do with number twenty-three, and those supposedly respectable spinsters who live there. He's almost certainly the one supplying knives to the maids too – after all, he sells daggers, sword canes and the like, and he's baseborn, and likely to consort with the lower classes. But lately, I'm seeing more signs that there's *ton* involved too. There's Wildenhall, in and out of there far more than a man buying accoutrements should be, for a start, but…"

He waited, baiting them, and they were caught, as he knew they would be.

"But what? What else - or is that who else?"

George leant in close, and spoke in a whisper.

"There's a woman – a Lady who's supposedly all purity and light – in her second Season, and never shown anyone any favour. But she keeps appearing at Bentick and Black… completely alone… and recently she's been seen at number twenty-three as well. So I don't think she's so morally upright and pure after all."

Interest lit their eyes, and he waited, sure that they would get suitably enraged.

"Well, Winthorpe – who is it? Tell us, so we can… take advantage… of that knowledge – if there's a soiled dove amongst that prim starched lot we have to socialise with, we'll be glad to entertain her."

He waited until they positively squirmed with needing to know, then whispered it.

"Lady Faith St John."

"No! You're gulling me, surely?"

"I'm not. Uppity piece acts all righteous and above a man, but all the while, she's tangled up in the things going on in Sackville Street."

"Outrageous! We'll see how she reacts when we make it obvious that we know what she's hiding. Perhaps a stroll in the gardens at the next Ball is on order…"

They all laughed coarsely. George was pleased, and spent the next half hour encouraging their outrage, and making sure that any new men who joined them heard about it too. They all drank steadily, and their group sense of outrage and self-righteousness grew in direct proportion to the amount they'd drunk. By the time George rolled home that night, he was certain that his agitating would pay off handsomely.

He only wished that he was in a position to receive an invitation to that next Ball they'd mentioned, so that he could see it play out for himself.

Lady Angela, a footman and a maid trailing her, as was only proper, even to walk a short way up the street, went up the steps of number twenty-three, and rapped the door knocker soundly. She glanced to each side, annoyed that dense lace drapes covered the windows, preventing her from seeing anything at all of what was inside. She waited, and, just as she was beginning to mutter to herself about rudeness, and no one answering the door, she heard footsteps inside. The door opened, and a most respectable looking butler stood before her, a footman behind him, to one side. The butler raised an enquiring eyebrow.

"Good Day, my Lady. How may I help you?"

She drew herself up.

"I am Lady Angela Heath. I've come to call on my dear friends, Lady Clara, and Lady Alarice. I do have the right house, I assume? This is their new abode?"

There was something about the butler's expression which gave Lady Angela the feeling that he regarded her as a nuisance, and she clenched her teeth. Really! The temerity of the lower classes! She waited, and the butler gave a little bow.

"Yes, my Lady, this is the correct house – or rather, one of them – Lady Clara lives next door, in number twenty-four. But, as the ladies are such close friends, there is a connecting door installed. If you will come into the visitors' parlour, I will let the ladies know that you are here."

He stepped back, and waved them into the house, leading them, as the footman closed the front door behind them, into a room almost immediately to the left of the entryway. The room was tasteful, but very plain, and Lady Angela pondered whether that was due to straightened circumstances, or a deliberate choice in decorating. She sat, and her maid and footman stood out of the way to one side. The butler left them there, closing the door after himself. She blew out a little huff of annoyance – it was obvious that she wasn't going to be given the chance to see anything of the interior of the house at all, beyond this room.

The mantel clock ticked as she waited, her annoyance growing. The plain room told her nothing about the inhabitants of the house – nothing more than she already knew, from having met them at the occasional soiree. After what felt like an hour, but was, according to the clock, merely five minutes, she heard footsteps approaching in the hallway.

The door opened, and the two women entered, both smiling as if utterly thrilled to see her. Lady Angela doubted that was the case. She stood as they came to her.

"Lady Angela, how delightful to see you! We've only recently settled in here - you are one of our first visitors. I've asked Bellshaw to send for tea."

"And cake. I do hope that you like cake?"

Lady Alarice had spoken first, then Lady Clara. Lady Angela maintained her smile, although she rather wanted to scream at the inanity of it.

"I do."

"Wonderful! Do be seated, so that we can have a little conversation. What brings you here?"

"Actually, I am your neighbour – I live on the other side of the street, towards the Piccadilly end. I thought it only right to call. We spinsters must stick together, mustn't we? Especially when there are so many... rumours.. wafting about lately."

Lady Clara and Lady Alarice exchanged a glance, then Lady Alarice spoke again.

"Rumours? I've not heard many lately – I choose not to indulge in egregious gossip."

Lady Angela considered her next words carefully – she did not, for one minute, believe that the women before her eschewed gossip – it would just need to be presented in the right way.

"Yes, rumours – rumours of young women where they shouldn't be, and of the possibility that a bawdy house is being set up in this very neighbourhood – shocking though that is."

The two ladies gasped, and their hands fluttered in shock.

"Oh my!"

There was a tap at the door, and the butler came in with a tea tray, which he carefully set down on the small table. As he did so, a peculiar 'thump' noise sounded, which seemed to come from the floor above. Lady Angela started slightly, but ladies Clara and Alarice behaved as if they hadn't heard it – were they deaf? Or ignoring it? Lady Angela said nothing – it would be most impolite to ask – but she frowned at the tea cup she was handed.

"It's terrible, isn't it? I can only hope it isn't true – that would lower the tone of the area to the point where I would have to consider moving. And so would you, no doubt?"

They shook their heads.

"No, no, I'm sure it can't be true, and it won't come to that. We like these houses too much to wish to move, especially as we've only just moved in! Let us not be concerned about unproven gossip."

"Are you sure it's utterly unproven? You haven't seen an unreasonable number of young women in this street? I'd even heard that more than a sensible number had been seen going to your servants' door."

They shook their heads.

"We were interviewing staff, and we are very particular, so we saw many before we chose the maids we took on, but beyond that, we've seen nothing out of the ordinary."

From above them, another thump occurred. Lady Angela narrowed her eyes – she didn't believe them, not entirely – but what could she do? She couldn't simply accuse them of lying. They spoke for another few minutes, about social events, and fashion, and then Lady Angela departed, even more curious than when she'd arrived. They had to be hiding something...

CHAPTER FIFTEEN

The moment that the door clicked shut, Clara dashed back into the parlour, and peeked around the edge of the curtain, watching to make sure that Lady Angela actually left. Only once she'd seen her reach a house down the street and enter it did she drop into a chair and meet Alarice's eyes.

"She's gone – I saw her go into her house."

A thump sounded from above, and they both burst into giggly laughter.

"Oh my! I thought she was going to drop her teacup the first time that happened. It was so hard to pretend that I hadn't heard a thing. And I absolutely couldn't look at you, or we both would have laughed then."

"We would, indeed. We must arrange for some thicker mats on the floor, or some other way to muffle the sound of them practicing. Do you think that we convinced her?"

Alarice shook her head.

"I don't – but she is at least confused, and unsure if we really are hiding something – that will have to be good enough, for now."

The bell on the door of the shop jingled, and Thomas stepped out through the curtain to stand behind the counter. Two young men were standing just inside the door, looking around as if they hadn't known what to expect when they came in.

They were dressed in the pink of fashion, obviously fops who thought themselves important.

"Can I help you, gentlemen?"

They started slightly, as if they hadn't noticed him, then drew themselves up with the bravado of the young and uncertain, striding up to the counter.

"We've heard that this shop can sell us something other than gentlemen's accoutrements, and we are interested in access to those... services – if the price is right, of course."

Thomas waited, but the men said nothing more. He considered their words – did the man refer to his trade in concealed daggers? It seemed highly unlikely, for what woman would tell a man like this about it? These were more likely to have been fended off at the point of one of his daggers than to have been told of them in good faith. Which left only one other possibility, given the rumours which had been circulating.

"Services? You'll have to be clearer, gentlemen – I don't know what you're talking about."

A glance passed between them, and one of them fidgeted, as if regretting being there. The one who had been speaking cleared his throat, then spoke again, in a rush.

"A woman's services! What else could I mean? Everyone's saying there's a new bawdy house around here, and that you're involved, you're the gatekeeper. We want in." Thomas laughed, and they both looked affronted, their faces reddening. "How dare you laugh at us! I should run you through for your impertinence!"

The man fumbled for the rather useless looking rapier he wore at his side, in a scabbard which was more decorative than functional.

Thomas reached down to the shelf below the counter, and curled his fingers around the hilt of the sword he kept there. Then, with a smooth movement, Thomas acted. He was so fast that the men saw nothing until the point of his sword came to rest, hovering where it just touched the front of the fop's waistcoat above his heart.

"I think not. This is my shop, and you can either leave now, and take your rudeness and your insinuations with you, or perhaps I will skewer you with this sword – which I can assure you is extremely sharp. After all, swords and sword canes are key parts of my business, so I've had to become very good at using them…"

The one who had been reaching for his rapier dropped his hand away from it, and they both took a large step backwards, their faces paling.

"I… ah… I take it that's a refusal to give us access…"

"There is nothing to give you access to. Gossip isn't necessarily truth. Now leave – and don't come back, unless you want to honestly purchase the type of goods you see around you in this shop."

To emphasis his point, Thomas lunged forward, the tip of his sword twitching quickly, so that the fob watch which dangled from a button on the man's coat dropped, with the button, to the floor. He pulled back, bringing the sword to rest – still in front of him and ready – and waited.

The fop spluttered again, quickly bent to scoop up the watch, then turned and marched out of the shop, his friend beside him.

Thomas sighed, shook his head, and returned the sword to its place beneath the counter. If the rumourmonger kept this up, he suspected that sword would see more use than it ever had before. He just wished he understood what whoever it was hoped to gain, by implicating him in their scandalous whispers.

That evening in a gambling den which was now very well known to him, George Winthorpe listened as two young fops complained bitterly about the uppitiness of the lower classes, and the fact that 'that shopkeeper in Sackville Street' wouldn't give them access to the new bawdy house.

George sympathised excessively, and said everything he could to increase their sense of outrage – this was playing right into his need to have Bentick and Black tarnished by scandal amongst the *ton*. It cost him more than he'd planned to spend, buying drinks for them, keeping them angry rather than thinking clearly, but he was sure it would be worth it.

As the night went on, they were joined by others, including Lord Charles Heath again, who promptly added his own complaints to the conversation, whining about the women of the *ton*, their painfully proper ways, and how they didn't know what was good for them, any more than the maids did. Eventually, all of them got to the point of talking about how anyone who thwarted them should be 'taught a lesson'.

At that point, before any of them remembered that he was a shopkeeper's son, George went home, well pleased with his efforts for the evening.

<<<<<O>>>>

From the moment they'd arrived, when a little flurry of whispers had immediately gone around the ballroom, Faith had known it would be a difficult evening. The older women were gossiping, and looking pointedly her way, and the young men also seemed to be whispering amongst themselves more than usual – and at times looking her way. It was only grim determination which kept her smiling, and pretending that she hadn't noticed any of it.

Lord Wildenhall was there, which was at least one good thing, and he had come to greet her early, and to secure a dance – the waltz, again, specifically. It gave her something to look forward to.

But as soon as he'd left her side, one of the rakish young fops had appeared beside her. She'd been introduced to Lord Charles Heath before, but had not danced with him – he and his set were really not the kind of gentlemen she wished to spend time with, and previously, they had seemed to understand that. But there he was, bowing exaggeratedly and asking her to dance. She had no polite way to refuse – not when she'd just granted Wildenhall a dance almost in front of Lord Charles, so she put on a false smile and declared herself delighted.

He stepped away from her, and Marion moved close and whispered to her.

"That's unusual – I wouldn't have thought you to be his type. He usually dances with the widows who are rather free with their favours, rather than the respectable young ladies."

"I know. I don't like him – but what could I do? I couldn't have refused him without creating a scene, could I?"

Marion shook her head, but still looked concerned.

"No, I don't suppose you could have."

At that point, the orchestra struck up, and the older gentleman who Faith was to dance with for the next set came to offer her his arm. She went with him willingly, for he was always the epitome of respectful and kind – but the oddness of Lord Charles having asked her to dance stayed with her, even as she danced with the other man.

The evening moved on, and still there were whispers and strange looks, although no one was quite brave enough to say anything to her face, for which she was grateful. Still, it was not an enjoyable way to spend the Ball. By the time Lord Charles appeared beside her, as the dancers began to form up for the dance she had granted him, she felt nervous, and rather frayed of temper. Were it not for the fact that her next dance after this one was to be with Wildenhall, she would have been tempted to tell Marion that she had a megrim, and ask that they go home.

"Our dance, Lady Faith."

She curtsied and placed her hand on his arm. As he led her away, his other hand came up to cover hers, and his fingers stroked a pattern on it in a way that was far too familiar to be polite. She gritted her teeth, and pretended she couldn't feel it.

They took their places in the line, and he kept hold of one of her hands, even though that was not required. His eyes met hers, and there was something in them she did not like – something of greed, and presumption, and more. Enough to make her shiver. When she did, he smiled, and bent forward to whisper in her ear.

"Anticipation, my Lady? How delightful."

She had no idea what he meant, but she did not like the tone of it at all. The dance progressed, and at every turn and twist, every point where the dance called for their hands to touch, he held on too long, too firmly, and when he released her hand, he trailed his across whatever part of her he could reach as he moved away.

She felt almost tarnished by his touch, as if it left a residue she wanted to wash off. As the dance was halfway through, and they reached the end of the line where they should turn and go back to the other end again, instead, before she realised what he was doing, he grasped her hand firmly, and pulled her the few extra steps to the terrace doors, and out of the ballroom.

"Lord Charles, what...?"

He kept going, almost dragging her down the steps into the garden, which featured a selection of curving hedges and hidden follies, and was barely lit by scattered paper lanterns. They rounded the corner of a hedge, which took them out of sight of the terrace, and Faith jerked against his grasp. He paused, and turned his face back to her for a moment.

"Don't act the innocent with me, Lady Faith. I know that you're morally wanting – delightfully so, from what I've heard – and that you've something to do with that new bawdy house on Sackville Street. So you can stop play acting, and be a good girl, and give me what I want – what others have already had."

Shock stole her breath, and she stumbled forward as he pulled her around the next hedge and into a gazebo like folly. He stopped in the deep shadows, and pulled her hard, spinning her into his arms, and brought his mouth down on hers, even as one hand slid up from her waist to her breast. His kiss was a slobbering distasteful mess, and his fumbling at her body revolted her.

She forced herself to release the tension in her body, to allow him to think that she was cooperating with his assault, and was rewarded by a loosening of the arm that pulled her against him.

It was all she needed.

She twisted then, forcing his grip looser, and sharply raised her knee, so that it collided very firmly with his most private parts, causing him to release her completely with a gasp, followed by him crumpling to the ground whilst cursing her in most colourful terms. Mentally, even as she hurried away, straightening her skirts, she stored up those words in her memory for later use.

She tidied her hair and clothes as she rounded the hedges, and sped towards the terrace as fast as she could walk, without looking as if anything unusual had happened.

The sound of cursing faded away behind her.

It was a pity, she thought, that the result of this would almost certainly be more gossip...

<<<<O>>>>

Thorne had spent the entire time from when he'd left Lady Faith after securing a dance, until now, as she danced the last dance before the one which was to be his, watching her. No matter how determined he was not to do so, his eyes sought her out, and he thought only of her, even when dancing with someone else. He feared he was poor company.

She was dancing now with Lord Charles Heath – a fop with a rakish wastrel's reputation, and it made him grind his teeth in frustration to have to see it. Heath didn't deserve her attention, and was, from what Thorne could see, being rather too free with his hands in the process of the dance. Thorne turned his eyes away, for the sight of it made him want to stride out there, pull the fool away from her, and plant him a facer.

Which was not the thing to do in a ballroom – especially as he had no right to defend her, no right to do anything, for there was nothing between them... well, beyond a few spectacular kisses.

Despite his intentions, he found himself turning back to look, again. His eyes sought her... and she wasn't there. He blinked, looking carefully, to be sure – but she definitely wasn't there, and the dance was only halfway through. His eyes followed the line of dance, to the end where the couples turned and came back to the start. That was close against the terrace doors.

One of which was slightly ajar. He was sure that it hadn't been before.

He was moving before any conscious thought was involved, hurrying around the edge of the ballroom and out through that door. He paused then, scanning the terrace, and finding no one. The garden, then.

He went down the steps and onto the path towards the first hedge, but was barely two steps along when he heard voices – one female, one male, sounding argumentative. He hurried. Then, from beyond another hedge, there came a choked half scream, and a stream of expletives worthy of a street thief.

Before he could turn around the next hedge, however, someone came from that direction, moving rapidly, and collided with him. He caught her, balancing them both before they could fall, and found himself holding Lady Faith. She tensed, then looked up and met his eyes. The tension left her, and she smiled at him, a little shakily.

"Lady Faith – what has happened?"

"Officially, nothing." She stepped back, took his hand, and near dragged him back towards the terrace. "You and I came out onto the terrace for a little air before our dance, as it's so stifling in the ballroom."

He allowed himself to be led.

"And actually?"

"Lord Charles stated that he knew that I was 'morally wanting' and therefore available, because I was associated with 'the bawdy house on Sackville Street'. He then proceeded to accost me. I rejected his unpleasant attentions in the most effective way available to me – by application of my knee."

Thorne failed to entirely repress the laughter which was his first reaction, and she turned her eyes up to him, as they reached the top of the steps. They stopped, standing in a perfectly respectable location, and he lifted his hands to her shoulders. She was shaking slightly, no doubt the reaction to what had just happened, but otherwise gave no sign that anything was wrong. Her strength and courage astounded him.

"He was not appreciative of your rejection, I could tell, if that was him I heard reciting a litany of impolite words?"

"That was him. Unfortunately, I suspect that this will only add more fuel to the fires of gossip which are attempting to burn away all that we have tried to do."

Thorne bent, then, and pressed a feather soft kiss to her lips, which she responded to for a moment, before they drew apart.

"We will weather this, somehow. And I can only offer you my highest regard. You have such well-honed skills in the use of certain concealed weapons..."

She laughed then, shaking her head at his choice of words.

"That was my first line of defence. Had he been foolish enough to still try to accost me further, then I have my 'sewing kit' in my reticule. I am sure that a sharp point applied in the right place would have been even more convincing."

"Indeed, I expect it would have been. But let us go back inside – I believe that I hear the orchestra striking up the waltz – I would not wish to miss our dance."

He bent again and pressed a soft kiss to her forehead as she sighed, then led her in through the terrace doors.

Against the first hedge below them in the gardens, Lord Charles Heath leant, still short of breath and in some pain, watching them.

"The deceitful cow! How dare she have the temerity to give out kisses to him, when she so roundly rejected me. The arrogance of her, and her near a spinster! She should be glad to have the attentions of a man like me, after she's been known to consort with whores and the like. She'll regret this, and so will he, I'll make sure of it."

CHAPTER SIXTEEN

Lady Angela Heath was standing, as was her habit, in a shadowed corner of the ballroom, nearly hidden by some potted palms, observing everyone. Only once she'd had her fill of taking note of anything of interest would she find a group of the best gossips, and join their conversation. She'd long ago discovered that lurking in dark corners often provided the chance to overhear other's conversations, when they thought themselves secluded. One learnt the most intriguing things that way.

The swirl of people moving around the ballroom had just brought a group of younger men to stand not far from her, on the other side of the potted palms. Curious, she leant in to listen to what they might say. The gossip of gentlemen was rarely as interesting as that of women, but still, one never knew what might be said.

"So, Heath, I saw that you managed to take the deceptive Lady Faith out into the gardens - how did you get on?"

She concentrated, suddenly interested more than usual – if she wasn't mistaken, the man who had just been addressed was her nephew, Charles. His voice came moments later, confirming that for her.

"The flighty piece had the audacity to reject my advances – forcibly."

The other men gasped.

"Forcibly? Whatever is the world coming to, that these women think they have the right to refuse us?"

"They don't know what's good for them – the woman's damned near a spinster – she should appreciate the attentions of a man like me – especially if she's involved with that bawdy house on Sackville Street we've been hearing about – she's lucky, after that, to have the attentions of any respectable man!"

"Indeed she is!"

Lord Charles took a breath, and went on, sounding more incensed by the moment.

"And there's more! She hurried off after... showing her unwise displeasure in my attentions... and, as she went, she met Wildenhall on the terrace – and let him kiss her. The temerity of her, to allow that, after rejecting my advances! I've a mind to make her pay – to make both of them pay."

As the other men muttered their aggrieved agreement, Lady Angela found herself as emotionally engaged as they were. How dare the girl reject her nephew! It didn't matter one whit that Charles had pressed his attentions on her in a manner which was, perhaps, not entirely as gentlemanly as it should have been – what mattered was that he had offered his attentions at all. Lady Angela had never, in the three Seasons she had endured before her father forbade her to have more, been given the gift of a gentleman's attentions – improper or not.

The chit didn't know what was good for her, refusing his attentions – she was, as the men had said, tantamount to a spinster – she should be glad that a man wanted her. Lady Angela was also pleased that the men thought Lady Faith involved in whatever dark deeds were going on in Sackville Street – she had suspected as much, after seeing the girl all alone on the street that day, but surely, if the men had heard such things, that confirmed it?

As the men wandered off towards the card room, still muttering about young women not knowing when they were well off, Lady Angela decided that it was time to leave the shadows, and seed some more gossip.

<<<<O>>>>

The next morning, Faith rose fairly late, after lying in bed replaying the events of the Ball in her mind. Could she have prevented Lord Charles from getting her into the gardens? Not really – at least not without creating a scene in the ballroom. But still, the fact that she had, again, applied a knee to a gentleman, was almost certainly going to filter out into the gossip – and that would come back to those close to her, inevitably.

She almost wanted to stay in bed for the day, to hide from that inevitability. Except that she knew it wouldn't work. There was nothing for it but to get up and face the day.

Later that morning, as she sat in the parlour, trying to decide exactly what to do, her mother came in, and settled onto the seat beside Faith, a serious expression on her face.

"Faith, I wanted to ask you… last night at the Ball, I heard some strange and troubling rumours – about you. Do you know anything about that…?"

Faith's stomach twisted with a mixture of fear, anger, and guilt. She couldn't tell her mother the truth – not after the scandals they had all endured the previous year – yet she hated lying about anything. She swallowed, searching for what she might say, and in the end, chose simplicity.

"I don't, Mother. I have no idea where it has come from – unless a gentleman whose inappropriate advances I rejected is being spiteful?"

Her mother shook her head sadly.

"I understand that you would not wish an association with a man who was improper in his attentions to you, but still… you need to find a husband, my dear. I want you to have the chance to be happy, not to be trapped in the life of a spinster!"

"I know that you do, and I am glad of your care, but I will not marry a man I cannot love, you know that."

Her mother nodded sadly, and said nothing more, but Faith knew that would not really be the end of it. Marion, who had come into the room as they were talking, regarded Faith closely, but said nothing. Faith was sure that she would ask her about it as well, later. She sighed, and returned her attention to the book she was supposedly reading. There was companionable silence for some time, until her mother spoke again.

"I plan to go out to make calls on various people today, and Marion is to come with me – will you accompany us, Faith?"

Faith shook her head.

"Not today, Mother. I am rather tired after the Ball, and want to rest. If I feel better, later in the day, I may make some calls myself – I will, of course, take a maid with me."

Her mother looked at her a little sharply.

"As you wish, my dear. You must make sure that you are rested, so that you can look your best at future events."

They lapsed into silence again, until, eventually, her mother rose and went to ready herself for her calls. As soon as she was out of the room, Marion hurried across and dropped onto the seat beside Faith.

"What happened, Faith? I can tell when you aren't giving your mother all of the truth…"

Unlike her mother, Marion would not be put off, Faith knew. There was nothing for it but to answer, with at least some of the details.

"I had cause to apply my knee in a strategic manner again, last night."

"Who was it this time?"

"Lord Charles Heath."

Marion frowned.

"But… he's not the sort I'd ever thought would approach you…"

"I didn't expect it, either. It makes no sense."

"No, it doesn't. He and the set he runs with usually spend their time with the widows who are free with their favours – I can't imagine why he might think you of similar ilk."

"Neither can I."

Except that she could, for he'd told her as much – but she wasn't going to tell Marion about that part of the gossip...

"Take care, Faith – as I said last time you felt it necessary to dissuade a gentleman in such a way, doing so risks your reputation, no matter how necessary it may be. People will twist such things, and turn them against you."

"I am very aware of that – but I refuse to be ruined in a garden by a pompous wastrel fop!"

"I cannot argue with that sentiment. Just take care. Now I'd best get ready to go with your mother."

With that, she rose and left the room. Faith went back to the book, and continued to fail to read it, until some minutes after she had heard the front door close, so that she was sure that her mother and Marion had actually gone out. Once she was certain, she hurried up to her room, dressed appropriately for making calls, then came down again and asked for the small carriage to be brought around.

She went to the Housekeepers office, and asked to take Janie with her, claiming that her lady's maid did not feel quite well. Once all was arranged, she waited fretfully in the parlour. She would go to call on Lady Prunella – for she needed to visit Sackville Street by the back lane, and find out if there was any other news about the strange gossip which seemed to surround them all.

And... perhaps... she might see Lord Wildenhall?

Thorne had slept badly, haunted by the events of the evening, caught between the memory of kissing Lady Faith yet again, and the anger he still nursed at the fact that Heath had felt entitled to attempt to treat her so. He wanted to seek the man out and make his opinion known in the most direct and physical way. It was madness, it was not his place to do it, yet he wanted it, badly. Almost as badly as he wanted to kiss Lady Faith, and more.

So, after breaking his fast, he went to Sackville Street, to see if Thomas had heard any more rumours, and to soothe his own feelings by seeing that what they had created was doing good, even if it was generating painful gossip.

He went into the shop by the front door, carrying his sword cane, determined to become used to having it by his side all the time – the previous night's events had emphasised for him the value that might present, should a Lady need assistance... Thomas looked at it with a smile as he entered.

"Are you getting used to it?"

"I am, although it's slow, and a few people I know have looked at me like I've gone a little mad, as I've never been one for affectations before. But I like the idea of having it with me."

"A little later, we can go up to number twenty-three, and you can practice – you look like you need to release some tension?"

"That I do. But if you don't mind, I'll just hide myself away in your back room for now. I came here to escape the conversation I might have been forced into at home."

"Certainly – I'm expecting a customer to collect some items, imminently, so that will work well."

Thorne slipped through the curtain behind the counter, and into the corridor. As he reached the door to the office, the back door opened, and someone came through, hurriedly, the momentary burst of bright light blinding Thorne to who it was.

They collided, and then he knew, instantly, that he held Lady Faith.

"Oh! I'm sorry, I…"

His sight adjusted, and he looked down into those clear blue eyes and smiled. His hands still rested on her shoulders, where he had caught her to steady her. Her voice trailed off, and she was simply smiling at him. He could feel his own smile spreading in response.

The scent of her surrounded him, and everything else faded away. He should release her, should step back, but he did neither. Instead, he pulled her gently towards him, and she came into his arms willingly, as if it was the most natural thing in the world. He pushed the office door open with his foot, and rotated them into the room. She laughed gently, her head resting against his shoulder, and reached out with her toe to push the door closed after them.

They stood there in the dimness of the little room, all alone, hearts pounding, until she tilted her head back to meet his eyes, and he, with a soft groan, bent to kiss her. It was a long, slow kiss, full of exploration, full of an appreciation of each other which they had, previously, never had time for. If anything, it seared his soul far deeper than those previous kisses had, and he revelled in the sensation.

When, after some minutes, they drew apart, neither spoke for some time, although her hand came up to gently cup his face, and he turned his head to press a soft kiss to her palm. She sighed then, and let her hand fall. The movement broke the moment, and it was as if time restarted itself.

"I… am sorry…"

"What for?"

Her voice was breathy – he wanted to kiss her again. He resisted.

"For what happened last night, for the gossip that seems to surround us, for the risk it all represents to your reputation… I am beginning to wonder if we should ever have started this enterprise in the first place. I never expected…."

She shook her head at him, her eyes bright with something – anger? Passion? Determination? He did not know.

"Don't be a goose, Wildenhall. Regardless of the gossip, what we are doing is a good thing, and I do not regret becoming involved. I am determined not to let a campaign of nasty gossip stop me from doing something which matters. At least you have the sense not to apologise for your kisses…"

He laughed then, and pulled her close again, just holding her.

"I could not apologise for the kisses – not and mean it – for I do not regret them in the least. Rather, I suspect that I am becoming quite addicted to kissing you…"

She smiled, and the smile lit her face to an extraordinary beauty, which utterly took his breath away.

"I cannot say that I am unhappy about that… quite the opposite. No matter how utterly improper it might be, I rather think the addiction is mutual."

A burst of unexpected joy filled him at those words, but he did not have time to consider that closely, for the door opened to reveal Thomas, who looked at the way they stood in each other's arms with a raised eyebrow, but made no comment.

"I've finished with that customer. I've closed the shop for a while, so that we can talk, or go up to number twenty-three for you to practice, if you wish."

Thorne stepped back a little, and felt all the colder for no longer having Lady Faith in his arms. Before he could say anything, Lady Faith spoke up.

"We need to talk – about the gossip, and what is happening. Wildenhall, did you tell Mr Black about last night?"

"No, I've had no chance – he was dealing with a customer."

She gave a nod, then turned to Thomas.

"Last night, at a Ball, a young man – I can't call him a gentleman – dragged me into the gardens and pushed himself on me with such improper persistence that I applied my knee to his privates with some force. He was convinced that I was wanton and available, because of gossip."

"Gossip? Which gossip?"

Lady Faith laughed.

"A good question indeed. He said that he had heard that I was 'associated with that new bawdy house on Sackville Street'. This is becoming very difficult – and I still don't understand why someone is starting these rumours."

Thomas shook his head, looking uncomfortable.

"I don't either – but I had two young fops come in here yesterday, demanding to be 'given access to the services reputed to be available here now'. And when I asked them to clarify, they said 'the new bawdy house'. When I told them I'd no idea what they were talking about, they blustered and went to draw rapiers on me. They soon discovered that I keep a sword to hand under the counter, and I am far faster than them. I cut the fob watch off the front one's outlandish attire, and sent them packing."

Thorne couldn't help but laugh at the image it raised in his mind.

"I know it' s not funny, but still..."

"It was rather amusing at the time, even whilst being worrying. I don't understand where its all coming from. Or why."

Lady Faith was looking thoughtful, and Thorne turned his attention back to her.

"What do you think, Lady Faith? Is this aimed at you, by someone who bears a grudge against you, for some reason? Although it seems extreme lengths to go to... and why they have connected you to here..."

She shook her head, her finger coming up to tap her lip.

"What if... what if it's not about me at all? What if I am just a convenient tool for what they want to achieve? Because I cannot think of anyone who has a reason to target me in this manner. But... if all of this is not about me, or you, Wildenhall, but is instead about Mr Black here, and his recent success, then perhaps it all makes more sense. Mr Black, is there anyone who could be said to have been disadvantaged, because you are doing well?"

Thorne stared at her, stunned. When she said it, it seemed so logical, why had he not considered such a thing before?

Thomas's expression matched his own.

"You think it's about me? That's… not something I'd considered. The only person who might possibly be worse off because of the increased custom I've had to the shop since Blackwater acknowledged me would be any person running a shop which sells similar products… But there are many of those, and I can't imagine that I've had an enormous effect on any one of them. I certainly have not intended to…"

"But perhaps you have had such an effect, nonetheless."

CHAPTER SEVENTEEN

The following morning, as he opened the shop, Thomas was still thinking about what Lady Faith had said. That he might be the cause of the dreadful gossip, just by existing and running his business was a most disturbing idea – but certainly not beyond the realms of possibility. He settled in to sit behind the counter, idly polishing things that were already quite well polished enough, when the door opened, and a man came in whom he'd seen a number of times before.

The man was no gentleman – he looked like a labourer, but his appearance was deceptive – Thomas knew that he worked for Lord Setford.

"What can I do for you today, John?"

"I'm not here to buy, today, Mr Black – that knife you made for me's still perfect. I wanted to ask you a question. Himself has me watching the street, since the strange gossip started, and I thought you might know something about the people who live along here."

"I do – some of them, anyway. Which ones do you need to know about?"

"Across the street – the place with a sign that says 'Winthorpe's Emporium – there's a younger man and an older man lives there. The young one – do you know anything about him?"

Thomas thought for a few moments.

"His name is... George. Mr George Winthorpe. He's the son of the older man. From what I've seen, George is a bit of a wastrel – he goes out and gambles, I'm told, and he doesn't seem to have much interest in the business, most of the time, despite the fact that he'll inherit it."

John nodded, and seemed about to ask another question, when Thomas held up a hand to stop him.

He couldn't believe that he hadn't thought of it yesterday. Winthorpe! The man was his closest competitor, being right across the road, and had always sneered at Thomas, from the moment that Mr Bentick had taken him on. Winthorpe had a very bad case of being 'superior', and in those days, his business had been far better patronised than Mr Bentick's, for Winthorpe's Emporium had been in existence for two hundred years or more, and had customers from the *ton* whose families had been patronising it for generations.

Customers who, in many cases, now shopped at Bentick and Black, since Blackwater had acknowledged Thomas as his half-brother.

"Is everything all right, Mr Black? You've gone a bit pale there."

"John, I've just had a realisation. Yesterday, I was talking with Lord Wildenhall and... another... about the gossip, and who might be doing it, and why. We were thinking that it was aimed at Wildenhall, and at a particular Lady of the *ton*, for reasons we didn't understand. But then, the other person suggested that maybe we were seeing it the wrong way, that maybe it was aimed at me, at my business. That perhaps someone was trying to create enough scandal to make the *ton* stop being willing to associate with me, to stop them buying from me. At the time, I couldn't think of anyone who'd benefit from that enough for it to be worth them starting all these rumours. But now... you've made me realise that Winthorpe might well be in that position – or perceive that he is."

"And if he thinks that way, if he thinks you've stolen the business that should be his, then he well might try to drive the *ton* away from you, and see scandal involving some of their own, and you, as the best way to do it."

Thomas nodded, his face grim.

"But what might he do, or get someone else to do, apart from inventing scurrilous stories about me, the shop, and those who associate with me?"

"From what I've heard, there's gossip suggesting that you're running a bawdy house and that Wildenhall is involved, as well as at least one society young woman. If the less scrupulous 'gentlemen' believe what they hear, who knows what they might try to do, to her, at least? If they ruin her, and blame it on her 'loose morals' and association with this shop… that sort of thing would be enough to make many of the *ton* turn away."

Nausea filled Thomas. The thought that Lady Faith could become the target of such a plan, all because she had chosen to support his endeavour and help young women learn to defend themselves horrified him. But what John had just said made sense, in a disgusting way, for the scandal of the corruption of one of their own would certainly make him a pariah in the eyes of the *ton*.

"Perhaps, if it's possible, Lord Setford might set more men to observe at larger Balls and Soirees, just in case anything happens?"

John nodded grimly.

"I'll ask himself if he would. I'm sure he'll think it's the right thing, when I tell him what we've just talked about."

<<<<O>>>>

George arrived at his favourite hell to discover Lord Charles Heath and his closest cronies already deep in their cups. They greeted him with enthusiasm, and handed him a drink. He settled in to discover what they were talking about.

"That uppity piece — how dare she! You've no idea just how much it hurt — she's got some strength in her, I'll give her that. But it's not to be borne — I'll make her pay, mark my words."

"Shocking, just shocking, Heath – to think that she acts so high and mighty when we all know where she's been going. Stands to reason she's a lightskirt, a trollop, and just hides it well, if she's been seen going in and out of that place, all alone. Black may pretend he knows nothing, but we know it's a front for a bawdy house, don't we?"

Lord Charles swigged his drink, then began expounding on the matter again.

"It is – and she proved how loose her morals are, straight after hitting me with that low blow – she met Wildenhall on the terrace and let him kiss her – why him, and not me, eh? What's he giving her for her favours?"

"A good question indeed. What do you plan to do about it, Heath?"

Lord Charles narrowed his eyes, and a sly, vicious grin crossed his face.

"I've been considering that. I'll need your help, some of you, at least. I'm thinking that, if one of you dances with her at Lord Halviston's Ball, and pulls her out into the gardens, I can be waiting there, with others of you. She can't drop all of us at once, now can she? We can overwhelm her, and have our way with her – if she's going to pretend to be all high and mighty and hold out on us, we'll just take what we want, and walk away. Then drop whispers in the ballroom afterwards, about what she's been doing. All her own fault for not cooperating to start with. She'll regret the day she spurned me."

The others muttered for a few moments, then nodded.

"All right. We can do that. Sounds like it could be a bit of fun – but we'd best work out who's going to dance with her now, so we know exactly what we're doing on the day."

They went on discussing it, but George said nothing. He had wanted a scandal, hadn't he? something big enough to make the *ton* turn away from Bentick and Black? Still, this didn't sit all that well with him – it would generate the requisite scandal all right, but he wasn't at all sure that he liked the idea of a young woman being treated like that, just because she'd rejected one man's advances.

He finished his drink and slipped away. There would be no gambling for him that night – he had no wish to be directly associated with whatever Heath and his cronies did.

<<<<O>>>>

Lord Halviston's town home was enormous, with the most extensive garden Faith had ever seen on a house in London. It was beautifully decorated, and the Ball was very well attended – this would be the last big Ball of the Season, for it was now June, and nearly everyone would soon depart for their country estates.

But the sheer number of people there had made the moment, when she first entered the room and, for a short while, all conversation stopped, quite the worst of her life.

Then others had arrived after her, and the attention of the crowd had been drawn away – but there had been whispers, and she had felt, all evening since then, excessively nervous. Perhaps it was also the effects of her little contretemps with Lord Charles Heath at the previous Ball – but regardless, it made her glad that this was the last time this Season she would have to attend any major event.

She had overheard, at least twice, the whisper of her own name as she passed people, and once or twice as well, whispers about Lord Wildenhall, and the suggestion of him being involved in distasteful activities. When he finally arrived, she noted that there was a similar momentary pause in conversation, followed by much whispering behind fans. She had just finished dancing with one of the older gentlemen whom she trusted, and, as he returned her to her mother, she watched Lord Wildenhall, hoping that he would come to her. The next dance was a waltz, and she had managed to keep it free, wishfully expecting that he might arrive in time to claim it.

"Good Evening, Lady Faith."

"Good Evening, Lord Wildenhall."

He smiled, his eyes full of their usual mischievousness, although she thought he looked somewhat strained.

"Might I dare to presume that you have this next dance free…"

He knew that she had kept it for him, she was quite sure, and she felt her cheeks heat a little, but defiantly met his eyes.

"You might, indeed, dare to presume…"

He grinned then, and offered her his arm to lead her to where the dancers were already forming up. He turned her into his arms, ready for the music to begin, and met her eyes. A small frown crossed his face.

"Are you quite well, Lady Faith?"

She sighed.

"I am, but I'm also somewhat uncomfortable. The gossip… they are talking about me – and about you – and none of it is pleasant, from what I have been able to overhear. It makes me wonder when someone will say something to my face. And when they do, I really don't know how I will respond."

"I don't know how I'll respond either, if someone challenges me about it. I suspect I'll just brazen it out, and look at them as if they are quite mad whilst confirming nothing."

She gave a small shaky laugh as the music started, and they began to move.

"I suppose you are right – but I don't like this at all. I am so glad that the Season is nearly over."

"So am I. But just for now, let us forget all about gossip, and simply enjoy dancing."

She nodded, and tried her hardest to forget everything except the feel of his arms around her – which, admittedly, was an intoxicating distraction. They said nothing more until the dance ended, and he escorted her back to where her mother stood, watching them, with a look in her eye which Faith thought was laden with matchmaking hopes.

Which was a concept that Faith did not wish to think too closely about at this time – not with so many other things to concern her.

Lord Wildenhall bowed, and stepped away. It took all her strength not to reach out and pull him back. He felt, she realised then, safe, a bulwark against the men like Lord Charles Heath, who had become, of late, something to be very wary of indeed. But she had no cause to detain him, so she had to simply watch him walk away.

"Faith dear, am I detecting some degree of… attachment… between you and Lord Wildenhall?"

She winced – what a time for her mother to decide to ask such a question! But, just as she struggled to find an answer, she was saved by the arrival of the man she was next to dance with – another of the younger set, who had never shown her any interest before. He bowed politely, and offered her his arm. Her mother stepped back, no doubt saving up that question for later, and Faith allowed herself to be led away.

The dance began, and, whilst he had little conversation, and his eyes roved her body in a manner which made her feel like he was imagining undressing her, his hands were not anywhere they shouldn't be, so she gave a little sigh of relief. Perhaps she would get through this evening successfully after all.

<<<<O>>>>

Thorne had retreated to one corner of the room, finding that he had no interest in conversation – indeed, he felt rather as if every eye was on him, and had Lady Faith not been in attendance, he might well have simply gone home to get away from it. He would not dance again that evening, and, on a whim, he went to the footman near the door and asked for his cane, which he had brought as part of his ongoing practice of getting used to carrying the thing. He took it, and went to stand in the shadows, leaning on the thing in as unconcerned a way as he could.

Looking natural with a cane was far harder than he had ever expected it to be!

He watched the dancers, his eyes, as always, going to Lady Faith. He wanted to be the one dancing with her, and the fact that he couldn't be, having already danced with her that evening, irritated him unreasonably. He envied other men every minute they had with her.

That thought made him become utterly still. It was true – he did envy others every moment of her company – when had he come to care so much? For he did care for her deeply, more so than he ever had for any woman. He swallowed, considering. The critical question, it seemed to him now, was – what was he going to do about it? And... did she care for him in equal measure?

His eyes followed her, automatically, longingly, through every step of the dance, until he could no longer bear it. He forced himself to turn away, to look at the rest of the room, to assess who was there, to take note of the little clusters of gossiping people. There were too many of those. He shuddered, and turned back towards the dance floor. The music had ended, and he searched for Lady Faith amongst those moving away.

She wasn't there. He looked again, sure that he must simply be missing her, that others perhaps obscured his view. But no, she wasn't there. A cold shiver of concern slid down his spine. Where had she gone? Surely, Heath wouldn't have tried again?

He swallowed, and moved towards the terrace doors, suddenly glad of the sword cane in his hand – one never knew...

<<<<O>>>>

The music stopped just as Faith and her partner reached the end of the line of dance, beside the terrace doors. He bowed, and tucked her hand through his arm, but then, as she went to step towards her mother, he gripped her tighter.

"I think not, my Lady. This way."

And with that, he hurried her out onto the terrace before she could exclaim her displeasure. She could not protest too violently as they stepped out, for to do so would cause a very visible scene – and the last thing she wanted this night was everyone's eyes on her, and more scandal! She could always apply her knee again, or pull out the concealed dagger from the reticule which dangled from her wrist.

"What do you think you're doing?"

She spoke firmly, but quietly. He laughed, pulling her towards the steps down into the garden, and she began to resist, to no avail.

"Why I'm making sure that you get what you deserve, you hoity-toity little whore."

<<<<O>>>>

In the ballroom, Lady Angela Heath smiled a rather predatory smile, her eyes on the closing terrace door. How interesting!

How many minutes should she allow, she wondered, before she went out into the garden for some air? And who should she take with her? Who would make the best witnesses to the no doubt scandalous scene they might discover in the garden?

She smiled. Lady Pittering, of course, and likely whoever she was talking to at this moment.

That decided, she turned and hurried around the ballroom, seeking Lady Pittering with all speed.

<<<<O>>>>

Faith gasped, nearly falling at the bottom of the steps, and attempting to use that movement as leverage to escape the man's grasp. It would have worked, if it were not for the fact that, as she did so, five other young men stepped out of the bushes and surrounded them, two gripping her arms and forcing her forward.

"Release me!"

They all laughed.

"Oh no, we won't be doing that – not until we've had what we want from you. You can't knee six of us at once, so you'll just behave like you should, and give us what you've been giving Wildenhall and others, all while pretending to be so pure."

The voice… it was Lord Charles Heath!

Shock held her silent, and for a moment she could barely breathe as they dragged her down a path into the tree-shrouded darkness. Damn Lord Halviston for having such a large garden! Her mind was in turmoil – surely there was something she could do? For if she could not save herself in some manner, she was doomed. They would have their way with her, and leave her ruined – they might abandon her then, or they might make sure that she was found with one of them, and forced to marry – perhaps if one of them wanted her dowry. Or they might release her, after ruining her, and then blackmail her…

The possibilities were near endless, and they were all bad.

She needed a miracle, and she was horrifyingly sure that she wasn't going to get one.

CHAPTER EIGHTEEN

Scattered around the garden, completely hidden in the shadows, a number of men watched, waiting to see if they would need to act. Lord Setford had impressed upon them how essential it was that they stay invisible if at all possible, so they would wait until it became clear that they had no option but to intervene. But they ground their teeth and clenched their fists at what they saw, each filled with the desire to plant a facer on one of the arrogant, obnoxious young men.

<<<<O>>>>

They reached a secluded spot, surrounded by hedges, where a seat had been placed beneath a tree, and Faith was relieved when they shoved her towards the bench, releasing her arms. They still surrounded her, making certain that she had no path to escape, but at least, with her arms free, she could, hopefully, get the concealed dagger out of her reticule. She stood there, with the tree and hedge before her, and the men behind her, and twisted her hands in her skirts, as if from fear – but that movement allowed her to open her reticule, pull out the sewing kit, and push the little button to release the dagger.

The men were arguing amongst themselves, about what they would do with her, and which of them would have the first opportunity to ravish her. She sobbed, but not because she had lost hope – far from it – she did it because she wanted them to believe that she would not fight them.

Not, she thought shakily, that she was likely to be able to hold them off for long, but still, even a little while might be enough, if she also screamed. No one was going to save her from them – not unless she managed to go at least halfway to saving herself.

She edged along the short distance to the end of the bench. Behind her, the argument stopped. It seemed that they had reached a decision. One of them moved closer to her, and she sensed the movement as he reached for her arm.

"We've decided, trollop, it's me you'll be servicing first. Now be a good girl and cooperate and..."

He had no chance to finish the sentence, for as his fingers brushed her arm, she spun, turning around the end of the bench, and putting it between them, even as she lashed out with the knife. She felt it connect with his sleeve, and cut through it to flesh, and she screamed then, not sure if it was from her own fear, from shock that she had cut a man, or simply from the hope of being heard.

He staggered back, swearing, and the others closed in.

"What is it, Heath, what did she... your arm... is that... blood?"

"It is – the nasty piece cut me, she got a knife from somewhere!"

There was a rumble of anger from all of them, and they moved closer, cautious, trying to encircle her, without getting cut. Fear filled her then, for she was certain that they would take that anger out on her, once they managed to trap her – which they surely would, soon.

She screamed again, then, desperate, hoping that someone, anyone, might hear.

Thorne scanned the terrace and, finding no one, hurried down into the gardens. He paused on the winding paths, unsure where to go in the overly large garden. As he did, voices came to him – a number of male voices, arguing, if he caught the tone of it aright – and behind that a sound which tore at his heart, the sound of a woman sobbing. He hurried on, letting the voices guide him.

Then, as he approached an arch through a hedge, the voices stopped, momentarily, then began again – a shout of anger, followed by a very feminine scream. He stepped forward, and peered through the archway, just as another scream echoed across the garden. What he saw made his heart near stop.

Lady Faith stood there, only the end of an old wooden bench between her and six men, a dagger in her hand. She moved it, threatening them, but they were closing in, and it was clear that she knew that she could not hold off six at once. A fierce anger filled him, even whilst his heart swelled with a kind of pride – he was astounded by her courage – and he drew his sword cane, glad now that he had brought it, that he had spent all those hours practicing.

He leapt forward, but not before the men had surged towards her, one of them slipping behind her and grabbing her arms. The men did not see him coming – they were all focused on Lady Faith, and the first they knew of his presence was when his sword point punctured the thigh muscle of the man trying to hold her. That man released his grip, falling to the ground, clutching at his leg, and Thorne went past him to stand with Lady Faith, almost back-to-back, his sword threatening.

The other men had stopped, frozen in place in shock.

Her voice split the sudden quiet.

"Well, that evens the odds a little."

She was shaky, but he could hear the determination in her words.

"It should be enough – but I don't trust that they have a grain of sense between them…"

She gave a half laugh.

"They are too full of lust for there to be any room left in their minds for sense."

"Indeed."

At that point, the men overcame their shock at Thorne's arrival and, all but the one whose thigh he had cut, came at them again.

"Wildenhall! You'll pay for this, as will your doxy. Serves her right for giving out to you, and playing too high and mighty for the likes of us."

One of them picked up a fallen branch the gardeners had missed, and moved in, obviously hoping to disarm Thorne, who did not, at that point, feel entirely confident, but he would fight until he could no longer move, if it saved Lady Faith from the fate these men had intended for her. For a short while, there was no sound but their heavy breathing, and the shuffle of feet on the ground. Thorne deflected the branch, again and again, and Lady Faith wove a glittering pattern in the air in front of her, the sharp tip of the dagger moving so that anyone trying to reach past it would almost certainly be cut.

But that was not, Thorne knew, a pace she would be able to keep up for long. As if confirming his thought, her voice came to him, uneven with the raggedness of her breathing.

"I think it's time for me to scream… again… and hope that… someone else… hears."

"Yes."

With that, she did so, issuing forth a piercing cry, which hurt Thorne's ears at that close proximity. Then, almost as if summoned by her hope, four large men stepped into the clearing. At first Thorne feared they had come to aid their attackers – but after a few moments, he recognised one of them. The man worked for Lord Setford. Now the odds were truly evened.

Setford's four men moved in, each tackling one of the attackers, and capturing them with efficient speed, whilst Thorne and Lady Faith continued to hold off the two closest to them.

Thorne kept fighting, with renewed energy now, hoping that soon, Setford's men would take down the one with the branch as well. He could not see what they were doing – after that first glance as they arrived, all of his concentration was on the man in front of him.

The man who, moments later, wasn't there anymore.

Thorne looked around, wiping his brow, and saw that all six were either bound and dropped on the grass like so much rubbish, or held firmly in Setford's men's hands. And beyond them, standing in the archway, he saw Lady Angela Heath, Lady Pittering, and two others of the *ton's* largest gossip circle. The expressions on their faces made him want to collapse into laughter, but the fact that Lady Faith sagged against him at that moment drew his attention to things far more important. He slipped his arm around her, and supported her.

Lady Pittering was spluttering, and one of the other ladies slid to the ground in a faint.

"What is the meaning of this? A young Lady, with a knife, fighting? Scandalous, utterly scandalous!"

Lady Angela said nothing, and Thorne watched her curiously, for her attention was not on Faith at all, but on one of the men bound at Setford's men's feet. He looked more closely. Ah... it was Lord Charles Heath. Given the name, he must be her relative. Well, well, this would be interesting.

"Release us! How dare you!"

The man who was protesting stopped speaking, very rapidly, when Thorne, after carefully ensuring that Faith could stand, stepped over to him, and rested the tip of his sword at his throat.

"I believe that you should not say another word, my Lord, given what you have been a party to, here, tonight. Your actions show you to be devoid of honour, and not deserving of any consideration."

Lady Pittering stepped forward then, ignoring Lady Angela as she helped the woman who had fainted.

"I do believe that we need to take this inside. An explanation can be made before everyone. I, for one, would most like to understand what happened here." She waved at Setford's men. "You – bring those young reprobates. And you, Lady Faith St John, have some explaining to do, as does Wildenhall. We can't have scandalous goings on like this at a Ball – it simply won't do. All of you – follow me."

With that, she simply turned, and walked off, back towards the terrace, fully expecting to be obeyed.

<<<<<O>>>>

Faith could feel a bubble of hysterical laughter rising within her, and when Wildenhall sheathed his sword and offered her his arm, for all the world like they were just taking a promenade in the park, she clung to him, making a small choking noise. His gaze came to her instantly, full of concern, but when she lifted a hand to her face and emitted strangled laughter again, his eyes filled with their usual mischievous delight in the world.

"This is obviously our penance for discussing scandalous things when we dance, my Lady." She pinched his arm, unable to speak without laughing. "Ouch! But... seriously, you need to get the laughter under control before we step into that ballroom. I rather suspect that this is going to be the scandal of the Season, and we need to be able to look serious. That was, after all, a very serious matter."

She nodded, and began taking slow deep breaths as they walked. He was impressed, yet again, at her strength – most women would have fainted away, yet she had drawn a knife on her attackers!

"How disreputable do I look, Wildenhall?"

He considered her, as they approached some lanterns.

"Your gown is torn in three places, your hair is utterly out of its pins, and you have a scratch on your face. You're beautiful."

"And you are obviously not quite in your right mind after all that exertion. Your coat shoulder seams have split, your waistcoat has lost most of its buttons, and you have a burgeoning bruise on your cheek. And you're perfect, just as you are."

He bent, hurriedly, and pressed a soft kiss to her brow.

"Remind me to kiss you properly, at the first available... private... opportunity."

They reached the steps, and went up onto the terrace, and followed Setford's men and their captives into the ballroom, where Lady Pittering had just waved the orchestra to a halt, and stepped onto the dais beside them. She raised her voice.

"Ladies and gentlemen, we have a most terrible scandal in our midst!"

Every eye in the room turned to them, where they stood. Faith swallowed, hard, but kept her chin up, and defiantly watched as whispers ran around the room at lightning speed.

"The gossip must be true – look who it is..."

"What did those men do, to be bound like prisoners?"

"It's Lady Faith – and look at the state of her gown! Shocking!"

"Is that a bruise on Lord Wildenhall's face?"

It went on and on, and Faith simply endured, watching as Lady Pittering and her friends revelled in the drama they had wrought.

Then the crowds parted, and Faith saw her brother, accompanied by Wildenhall's father, the Duke of Elbury, step out of the gap. Drummond came to her, and reached out a gentle finger to touch her cheek.

"What happened here, Faith?"

The breath she hadn't known she was holding left her in a rush of relief. He wasn't angry with her, he wasn't making assumptions, no matter how bad it looked. She realised then that Wildenhall still held her arm, and the warmth of his touch was equally reassuring.

"Those men," she pointed at the six bound captives, "collaborated to drag me into the gardens, with the intent of ravishing me. They told me as much. Had I not had my small knife," she lifted it, only then realising that it was still in her hand, "they would have succeeded, before Lord Wildenhall reached me, and helped hold them off. Even then, it was only the assistance of these gentlemen which saved both of us."

She had indicated Setford's men, and Drummond's brows rose, for he had seen some of these men before, and knew, immediately, whose they were. One, she realised now, was dressed as a footman, and had likely been slipped in among Lord Halviston's staff by Setford. At her words, there was an immediate uproar in the room, including denials from the attackers, and exclamations of disbelief from their friends and families. When it did not die down quickly, the Duke of Elbury turned to Wildenhall.

"Is all that Lady Faith has said true?"

"It is, Father."

The Duke nodded, then turned back to face the room. He took a very deep breath, and spoke one word, at enormous volume – a volume which would not have gone astray on a battlefield, or on the stage.

"Silence!" It achieved its purpose. A shocked stillness arrested the room. He smiled. "Thank you." Then he turned to the bound men. "You – you will tell me – one at a time, why you acted as you did, and why you thought that your actions might be remotely acceptable."

Despite his instruction, they all tried to speak at once.

The Duke pointed at one of them, and Setford's men cuffed the others into silence.

"We were told she was a trollop, that she was involved with the new bawdy house everyone says is on Sackville Street somewhere, and with the fact that all these maids have started to carry knives. She's been seen all alone, places a respectable woman shouldn't be, so of course we believed it! Everyone was saying it."

"And just who is 'everyone'?"

The man blanched, and angled his head towards Lady Pittering and her coterie.

"They've been whispering about it, for a start!" That got shocked gasps from Lady Pittering and Lady Angela, who promptly fainted. "But there's been men's gossip too."

Behind the drama of the questioning, one of Setford's men stepped towards a gentleman who stood watching, and quietly spoke to him. The gentleman, who was the Marquess of Canterford, looked startled, then pleased, and sent Setford's man back to his guard duty with a smile.

The Duke of Elbury continued his questioning, following the attackers comment about men's gossip.

"And where did that come from?"

"I believe that I can cast light on that."

The voice was unexpected, and Faith looked around to discover the Marquess of Canterford, who was married to one of Wildenhall's sisters. The Duke looked to him with a raised eyebrow.

"You can?"

"Yes. It's been reported to me by a number of people that they'd overheard some odd conversations in gambling dens of late – conversations where the son of a man who is a business rival to Mr Thomas Black, was feeding stories to young men about women with weapons, bawdy houses and more – all, once it is considered together, with the intent of discrediting Mr Thomas Black's business, and causing the *ton* to no longer buy from him. Not that the young men who've been fed these stories seem to have realised that to be the intent. As far as I've been able to ascertain, it has almost all been complete fabrication, born of petty viciousness and envy. It would appear that these young men before us chose to simply believe everything they heard, rather than validating it..."

The bound men had all gone rather pale at his words.

One of them stuttered, forcing words out.

"Fab… fabrication? All of it? But no, surely not – there are maids with knives, I swear – knives like that one."

He pointed to the knife in Faith's hand.

A flurry of whispers went around the room, and one of Lady Pittering's friends spoke up.

"And we've heard that she," she pointed to Faith, "has been seen going into Mr Black's shop, far more often than a Lady could have reason to go to a Gentleman's Outfitter's. And alone, too!"

The woman beside her nodded.

"Yes – surely no self-respecting woman would do such a thing. It must be a front for a house of ill-repute, or the like!"

The Duke frowned, and seemed about to say something, but Faith could stand it no longer – now that they had all spoken, it seemed so utterly silly that the situation had come to this, that she should have spent so long fearing the gossip.

After all, what they were doing with number twenty-three was so much the opposite of a bawdy house that she could not imagine anything further removed from the idea.

She burst into laughter, clinging to Wildenhall's arm, as the ludicrous nature of the situation overwhelmed her.

CHAPTER NINETEEN

A whole new depth of shocked silence stilled the room, and Faith's laughter echoed through it. She struggled to stop, to stand straight and compose herself, but for a short while, it eluded her and only when her brother gently took her arm did the laughter come to a hiccupping stop.

"My dear sister, would you do everyone the courtesy of explaining what has caused you to laugh so, in the midst of such a serious situation?"

His voice was kind, but held an undertone of desperation, and Faith knew that he hoped for some magical way to end this dreadful public spectacle. She breathed deeply, steadying herself, hastily seeking the right words. Wildenhall's hand held hers, she realised then, for she had gripped it when the laughter had overtaken her. He squeezed her fingers, and she looked up, meeting his eyes. Their hazel depths were full of amusement, and an understanding of what had made her laugh. It was enough to give her confidence, and she turned then to her brother and the Duke of Elbury, who both waited with admirable patience.

"I do apologise for my laughter. I was simply overcome by the absurdity of the situation – for, although I was most definitely endangered, the reasoning for that, which these men have given, is a very large distortion of the truth."

The Duke raised an eyebrow at that.

"And that is cause for laughter?"

"Indeed, it is. Let me explain, as simply as I can. It all began with Mr Thomas Black, and daggers like this." She lifted the dagger, which was still clutched in her hand, momentarily wondering how she had managed not to cut Wildenhall when the laughter had taken her. A small flurry of sound went around the room at her words. "This dagger is special – let me show you." She released Wildenhall's hand, reached into her reticule, and pulled out the sewing kit. "It can be sheathed in this sewing kit, and once there, cannot be detected, unless one knows exactly where to press to release it." She demonstrated as she spoke, and a series of gasps resulted. "Daggers such as this are designed for ladies to carry, so that, if pressed, they have a way to defend themselves against inappropriate advances."

The Duke nodded.

"That seems a useful innovation – but what has it to do with the attack on you this evening, and your laughter?"

"Mr Black began making these for maids, and women of the lower classes in general, for they are frequently at risk, and he wished to help prevent the harm which can come to them. But then he realised that he would need to teach them how to use them to best effect, if they were to be truly useful. Most men will pause when facing a dagger, and even more so, if the wielder appears to know what they are doing. So he decided that he wished to establish a self defence school for young women. A school specifically to help prevent situations in which women would be forced onto the streets, and thence into bawdy houses, simply to survive."

At those words, there was a collective intake of breath in the room, as people began to see the point of the matter. The Duke now had the beginning of a broad smile.

"I begin to see, perhaps, the cause of your laughter."

"Yes – all of this gossip about the activity near Mr Black's shop being because of a bawdy house, when that is the furthest thing possible from what was actually happening, led to my laughter."

"I can see the absurdity of it, when you describe it that way. But… how did you come to know of this, and to have one of the daggers? And what has Wildenhall got to do with it, apart from coming to your aid this evening?"

Faith took a very deep breath – for here was the point where her own behaviour would be called into question, and some of what she needed to admit to was, in the sense of society's expectations, unforgiveable. But she had gone this far – she would not stop, would not let the gossips win.

"I came to know of it because a maid in our household had one of the daggers, and after I had a bad experience at a Ball, where a gentleman pressed himself upon me inappropriately, and I barely escaped him, she showed it to me. I realised immediately that young ladies of the *ton* needed such things, and the skills to use them, just as much as a servant might. The events of this evening have made that very clear. If I had not had this dagger, I would have been overcome by those six men, well before anyone could have reached me to help me. I would have been ravished in these very gardens."

Shocked gasps filled the room.

"You make a valid point."

It was her brother who spoke, and he looked at the bound men with an expression that reminded Faith of his past as a privateer – that expression said that, were it up to him, they would suffer at the point of his sword.

"After my maid told me of it, I went to Mr Black's shop – surreptitiously, I admit – to order a dagger."

At that point, Wildenhall spoke up.

"And when collecting her dagger from his shop, she happened to be there at the same time as I was. I had, a few weeks earlier, decided that I wished to obtain a sword cane, and learn how to use it – something I was most glad of this evening, when it allowed me to help Lady Faith to defend herself."

He lifted the cane, and slipped the sword part way out of it, to more gasps.

The Duke frowned.

"I had the impression that you were more involved than that…"

"I was, I am. After discussion with Mr Black, I chose to become his partner in this endeavour. I have seven sisters – and as each came of age to come out into society, I made quite certain that she knew how to protect herself. So I deeply sympathised with Mr Black's aims. My accidental meeting with Lady Faith led to her asking more questions, and wishing to assist."

Faith raised her voice over the scatter of conversations which had begun in the room.

"And I, once I understood the possibilities, chose to invest the funds which I had saved into this venture, with the hope that it might be expanded to provide lessons to young ladies of the *ton*, as well as their maids."

That caused more whispering, but to Faith's ear, much of it sounded more approving than not. Wildenhall spoke again, causing the whispers to stop as people paid attention.

"I arranged the purchase of two houses further up Sackville Street – in which respectable spinster Lady tenants now live, but some rooms of which are used to teach the women who buy daggers how to use them, as well as how to protect themselves without daggers if necessary. So all of this 'extra traffic of women' that has been blown up into apparently scandalous gossip, based purely on guesses about what was happening, has resulted from women taking action to learn how to protect themselves. That was not something which I, or Mr Black, could have predicted, of course."

Faith nodded then, and cleared her throat.

"We were puzzled as gossip began to grow, and I was afraid that something like what happened this evening would occur. We could not understand where the gossip was coming from, or why. Certainly, my purchasing something from a Gentleman's Outfitters was unusual, but not so much that I thought such gossip would occur. But now, it has become clear that Wildenhall and I have merely been used as part of a larger plan."

"What plan?"

"A concerted effort by Mr Black's commercial competitor to discredit his business, by the association to scandals, so that all of you would stop buying from him. Regardless of what you choose to think of me, I would ask that you do not let that underhanded competitor achieve his aims. I would ask that you continue to give Mr Black your custom."

Wildenhall spoke into the small silence that followed.

"And I would ask that you allow your daughters to learn how to defend themselves, so that there is never a moment when your daughter stands in a ballroom as Lady Faith does now, having suffered the unwanted attentions of a gentleman who should know better."

That caused a stir. The six bound men shrank in on themselves, as if wishing to sink through the floor and disappear, knowing full well that their reputations were utterly destroyed. Lady Angela Heath and Lady Pittering shrank back, as if trying to be invisible. After a short while, the Duke of Elbury smiled at Wildenhall, and Faith felt certain in that moment that he was proud of his son. Then he lifted his hands, and clapped them together loudly. People turned to him, and he continued to clap.

"I applaud what has been said – I applaud this venture, which aims to help protect the vulnerable. I will choose to add my own donations to keeping this school in existence, as I would donate to any other charitable endeavour designed to give poor young women a better life, and wealthy young women greater security – and I would suggest that many of you might be well placed to do the same."

Faith watched as her brother lifted his hands, and joined the Duke in applauding them. Moments later, a wave of applause ran around the room, for no one wanted to appear to disagree with the Duke, or to appear miserly. She felt light-headed, and wondered, then, if she was going to swoon – something she had never done!

Wildenhall's hand sought hers again, and she took strength from that contact, managing to simply stand there, and take in what they had achieved.

<<<<O>>>>

The following morning, Faith woke slowly, discovering that she ached all over. Fending off her attackers had taken a far greater toll on her than she'd realised at the time. Meg, on hearing her groan, came into the room to help her dress, and soon she was ready to brave going downstairs, where she was certain that her mother would have dozens of questions, and remonstrances, for her. The thought was enough to make her want to groan again, for a completely different reason.

Still, she forced a smile onto her face, and went down to the breakfast room. Perhaps food would help.

She stepped into the breakfast room, and everyone looked up. She swallowed then, unsure.

"Do come and break your fast, Faith, you look positively pale and shaky."

Her mother sounded more concerned than anything else — that was a relief. She went to the sideboard and filled a plate, then settled at the table. Drummond lifted the newspaper which lay beside him, and handed it to her.

"You're the sensation of the day, Faith. The gossip columns are full of it." Her stomach contracted, and she suddenly wasn't at all sure that she could face eating. Drummond went on as if it was all perfectly ordinary. "It's not all bad. A few of them are offended by your 'lack of propriety', but most are cautiously approving of the whole school concept, and many are more focussed on making sure that your attackers' reputations are as destroyed as possible. Over all, I think you've come out of it well."

A degree of relief slipped into her, and she assayed a bite of toast and marmalade. It tasted good, and her nerves steadied. Then her mother spoke again.

"Why on earth didn't you tell us?"

The toast immediately seemed to taste of dust.

She forced herself to swallow. This was no time to be meek – she knew that if she didn't stand up for herself, she'd never hear the end of it.

"I didn't tell you, because I knew that you would disapprove of my going there, and of my learning 'unladylike' things. But I wasn't going to give up the chance – it was too important an endeavour. But, mostly, I thought that I could keep people unaware of it, at least for quite some time. I didn't want to expose the family to more scandal, not after last year...." She shook her head and gave a small self-deprecating laugh. "I rather failed there, in quite the dramatic fashion, didn't I?"

Drummond gave a small grimace, but shook his head.

"I hardly think this compares, especially as the end result, at least so far, appears to be tending towards positive. Still, I suppose we won't know until we go to Lady Charterwood's Soiree this evening."

Faith shuddered at the thought, but knew that it was necessary. The *ton* would either give her the cut direct, or they would behave as if nothing was wrong, probably whilst sidling up to her and asking her to tell them all about it.

"I suppose you're right. We will see how they all treat me."

With that, they left discussion of it alone, and Faith managed to eat enough to feel at least reasonable. Then she took herself to the library, curled up in her favourite chair, and tried to read. The book ended up abandoned on her lap, and instead, she simply stared at the shelves before her, replaying the previous night's events in her mind.

Especially the moments when Lord Wildenhall had stood back-to-back with her, fending off her attackers. Just his presence had given her the strength to keep going, and the memory of him supporting her afterwards, of him holding her hand, filled her body with warmth now. She remembered the times that he'd kissed her, and her fingers drifted up to her lips as she did. She wanted to spend time with him, wanted to touch him, wanted to be kissed by him. But the Season was nearly at an end, and now all they had done was scandalously in the eye of the *ton*. Would she still be able to see him? Or would the scandal force them apart?

That thought was like a knife to her heart, and she drew a sharp intake of breath. She simply could not bear the idea of being separated from him for weeks or months! She could not, she realised, bear the thought of being separated from him... at all...

She had shocked herself with that realisation and now, with nothing else to distract her from it, she had no choice but to consider, truly consider, the implications.

She had come to care for him, deeply. So deeply that she was tempted to contemplate the word love... Did she love him? She suspected that she did. And if that was the case, the question which echoed through her mind was simple, yet the most important one of her life.

Did he love her?

<<<<O>>>>

Thorne stared out of the Elbury House parlour window, much as he had done barely two months earlier, and with much the same sense of irritation.

Outside, the day was perfect, as summer brought warmth, perfect flowers, and brilliant sunshine, but inside, a pall hung over his thoughts. Behind him, scattered over the couch where he had been sitting, a collection of the days newssheets proclaimed the events of the previous evening, in various degrees of shocked and over dramatized prose.

It left him utterly uncertain how he might be received in society, and what impact all of it might have on his family. And no matter how much he wished to protect his family from censure, he knew that he couldn't – and worse, he knew that, if the price of doing so was to give up the venture of the self-defence school, he wouldn't do it. The school was too important to allow society to force it to stop.

But if he insisted on continuing being scandalous, would Lady Faith turn aside from him? Would her family insist that she did?

It was not a thought that he could bear.

He went back and stared at the gossip columns again – at least a number of them were positive about the venture itself, mainly, he was sure, because of his father's choice to speak out in support last evening, in the ballroom – but would that be enough?

His mind kept coming back to the events of last night, to the moment when he had seen Lady Faith surrounded, defending herself. To standing back-to-back with her, fending off her attackers, to supporting her as they went back into the ballroom, to her courage in the face of it all, to the feel of her hand in his, to the trust in her eyes when she looked at him. To the way that he had felt, where he had not wanted to release her hand, where he had wanted, instead, to pull her close and kiss her, right there, in the middle of a crowded ballroom where every eye was upon them.

He wanted to kiss her now.

He wanted to kiss her every day.

But that would mean being with her every day. His breath came short. The implication was undeniable. There was only one way in which he could be with her every day.

And that was to marry her.

He loved her.

But did she love him?

There was only one way to find out. He rose, just as his father walked into the room.

"Where are you off to?"

"To ask the most important question of my life."

<<<<O>>>>

"Lord Wildenhall."

Faith looked up at the butler's announcement, her heart pounding as she hurriedly set the book aside, uncurled herself from the chair, and stepped forward to greet him. Why had he come?

"Good day, Lord Wildenhall, this is a delightful surprise."

Behind him, she could see that the door was still open, and that Marks lurked discreetly where he could see into the room – giving them some privacy whilst serving propriety. Wildenhall took her hand and bowed. Then, without releasing it, he simply stood there, his eyes meeting hers, as an awkward silence extended. Just as she was about to say something, he finally spoke.

"I... after last night... I couldn't..."

Uncharacteristically, he appeared to run out of words. Faith frowned, totally unsure herself, then chose to be direct.

"After last night, indeed. I've no idea what society may do, but I think a more important question is 'what do we do now'?"

It was enough to make him smile, to make him relax, in some manner, to bring the cheerful mischief back to his eyes, and she felt her own tension fade away as a result.

"Scandalise them all again, by doing something they think is proper? After all, surely that's the last thing they'll expect from us."

What did he mean? Could it be...?

"Just what proper thing are you suggesting?"

"Ah, I was rather hoping that you might agree to marry me?"

For a moment, she was dizzy, her mouth dry, but just for a moment.

"Yes. But... only if you don't expect me to be a 'proper little wife' after that. I refuse to give up learning to fight – but I think a rapier should be next...

"Of course – having a wife who can guard one's back – literally – seems like a most admirable plan."

EPILOGUE

Four weeks later

Thorne's father had looked at him when he had returned from proposing to Faith, and informed the Duke of it, with an amused and long suffering expression. He'd asked the question which he had asked each of his daughters suitors.

"Do you love her?"

And Thorne had laughed.

"Of course I do, or I wouldn't have asked her."

"Good. Now go and tell your mother. It seems that you are the only one of our children to do things in anything close to the normal manner, but she will still be annoyed with you, for doing this in summer, when everyone's likely to be out of town."

He had simply laughed, and gone to find his mother as commanded.

Now, four weeks later, after much frenetic wedding planning by the Duchess and Lady Hungerwood, the day had arrived. That was rather a relief – wedding planning was a special kind of torture.

For a summer wedding in London, the church was crowded, with some of the *ton* having even come back to town for a week, just to see the wedding of the two involved in the scandal of the Season. Thorne and Faith found it all rather amusing, now that the first flush of fuss about it had faded.

Mr Swithin had set up the school as a charitable institution, and donations from various doyennes of society were steadily flowing in. What might have ruined Faith had, it seemed, instead made her famous, and admired by many.

It made their wedding day all the better.

Thomas Black stood up with Thorne, and Marion with Faith. The words were spoken in the sanctity of the church, and a great sense of peace filled Faith as she turned, her hand on Thorne's arm, and they walked out into the summer sunshine. Many people waited to congratulate them, but the ones who mattered most were not the nobility, but the long line of women who were quite obviously servants or poor women. They all stood quietly, smiling, each with a hand on a reticule, or in their pockets. To the casual observer, they simply waited to see the happy couple pass by.

But Faith and Thorne knew differently.

This was an honour guard, and a very special one.

Each reticule and pocket contained a concealed weapon, encased in a sewing kit or the like. Their presence was the best gift that anyone could have offered.

Back at Hungerwood House, the Wedding Breakfast was sumptuous, and people clustered together, talking as they ate, or danced with some enthusiasm, and then collapsed, fanning themselves as the summer heat near overwhelmed them. Faith had pulled Thorne to some chairs in one corner, and simply sat, hoping that no one would come to talk to them, at least for a while.

"How early do you think we can sneak away?"

Faith's fingers tangled with Thorne's as she spoke.

He bent and brushed a soft kiss to her forehead, and heat filled her. She wished that she might turn her head up and look for a far deeper kiss, but she resisted the temptation. He laughed softly.

"I suspect that our mothers would be deeply offended if we did not stay until at least very late afternoon. It will come soon enough. And our new house is not far."

The Duke of Elbury had taken a very sensible approach to the concept of giving a wedding gift, and purchased an excellent townhome for them, which was located almost equidistant between Elbury House and Hungerwood House. The newly named Wildenhall House had been hastily prepared – at least to a state ready to receive them for the next few days. Staffing it had been easy, for they had simply asked among the students of the school and their families. Still, fully setting up a London home for the heir to a Duke was no simple matter, so they had decided to go to the country, to Wilden Chase for two weeks, as a wedding trip, so that the townhome would be fully prepared once they returned.

Faith leant against Thorne's shoulder, just watching all of the people in the room. Her mind was full of happiness, and she still marvelled at how it had all turned out.

"I am so happy, right now.

Thorne slipped an arm around her, and bent to whisper in her ear.

"Good. But I intend to make sure, later today, that you are happier again – happier than you have ever been in your life."

Mid-October 1820

"Will that do my Lord?"

Thorne stepped back and regarded the front of number twenty-three Sackville Street. To one side of the door, an elegant and discreet sign had been affixed to the wall.

THE WILDENHALL ACADEMY OF SELF-DEFENCE
FOR YOUNG LADIES.

"Yes, that's excellent. I do believe we've finally got it exactly straight."

"Very well, my Lord, I'll make the final fixings then."

The man set about it, and Thorne turned to Faith, smiling.

"Are you happy?"

"Very much so. And we've got a long list of applicants to be students, both of the aristocracy, and of the lower classes. We need to train more of the early students to be teachers, or we'll never keep up."

Thorne tucked her hand over his arm, and they walked back down the street to number thirteen, and stepped into Thomas' shop.

"Speaking of keeping up with the demand... Thomas, how goes your search for an apprentice?"

Thomas Black set aside the dagger he was polishing and grinned.

"Very well – I think I've found the right one – the brother of one of the maids – he's already got a deft touch, and I don't think he'll be too hard to teach. And in the meantime, I've thoroughly solved the Winthorpe problem."

Thorne raised an eyebrow.

"You have? How?"

"I've come to an arrangement with the elder Winthorpe – I've subcontracted him to manufacture a whole range of items that I sell, but which I have little interest in making myself. He does quality work, so I have no problem with that. His business will survive, and my life will be easier. The influx of business since the dramatic events at that last Ball of the Season has been quite excessive, so I'm glad of the help."

Beside him, Faith frowned.

"But what of the younger Winthorpe – the gambling spreader of gossip?"

Thomas laughed.

"I've conspired with his father. I'm paying George for advertising. It's enough of a payment that he can gamble a little, and all I'm asking is that he keeps spreading gossip – but this time, gossip about how good our products are, and how talented the students of the school have become. It serves two purposes – the young rakes of the *ton* will think twice about accosting their servants, and they'll think of us first when they want to buy gentlemen's accoutrements."

"That's wonderful!"

"I think so – we'll see how well it works out. But for now, before we sit down and plan the next steps for the school, I've got your rapier ready, Faith."

"Oh! Let me see..."

Thomas set it on the counter, and all three of them bent over it, examining the beautiful craftsmanship, all thought of past scandal forgotten.

The End

I hope that you enjoyed 'A Heart for an Heir'.

You'll find a preview of the first book in this series

'A Spinster for a Spy'

After the About the Author section of this book.

AUTHOR'S NOTE

- As always, there are a lot of things in this story which actually existed. In many cases I take a little bit or artistic licence with things – sometimes the timeline, and sometimes the exact structure of things. In this particular book, the main aspect is that Swallow Street and Sackville Street existed (and still do today). The street numbers that I have given are the real street numbers on Sackville Street then. But the interesting thing is that the numbers didn't work like street numbers do now. Now, street numbers are odd on one side of the road, and even on the other. Back then, the numbers went up one side of the road, and back down the other.

- The history I give at the start of chapter four, of twenty-three and twenty-four is real. You can discover more about Sackville Street, what the houses were like, and who lived in it when, here - https://www.british-history.ac.uk/survey-london/vols31-2/pt2/pp342-366#h3-0013 and more about Swallow Street here - https://www.british-history.ac.uk/survey-london/vols31-2/pt2/pp57-67

- The two images following show you the area, with the house blocks, (and on the earlier one, the house numbers). Between 1816 and 1819, the Regent Street Quadrant was built. That involved knocking down a lot of what had been Swallow Street. Only a small amount of it was left at the Piccadilly end. The curve marked on the first map is the location that became the Regent Street Quadrant. This is pre 1816. The second map is 1870.

- As this story is set in 1820, the Regent Street Quadrant is newly built, and the area behind the curve at the upper end of that block of Swallow Street is mostly gone, with only stable buildings and the like remaining as part of a lane behind the top end of Sackville Street. As we can't know exactly what it looked like at that time, I have taken an artistic licence approach to how I think it might have been, for story purposes.

Leicester Street
VIGO LANE
Glasshouse Str
PICCADILLY
ngton House

Vigo Street
Sackville Street
Swallow Street
Chapel
Piccadilly Place
Great Vine Street
Regent Street
School
Vine Street
St James's Hall
Piccadilly

- I've also taken an artistic licence approach re Lady Prunella's house being number 11 Swallow Street, given that 9, 10 and 11, as they were then, actually got knocked down for the building of the Quadrant, but I am pretending they survived, and number 12 was the first of the knocked down ones – you can see the house numbers on the map on the previous page to see what I mean. The reason I am doing this is because, in book 4 of this series (A Diamond for a Duke) I had made it number 11, as that was a best guess based on the maps I had available at the time – I hadn't found the one I got that image from on the previous page yet. So for consistency within the series, it's number 11.

- You may also have wondered about the amount of the rent that Thorne offers numbers twenty-three and twenty-four to Ladies Clara and Alarice for.

   You can discover more about rental costs in London in the early 1800s here - https://alexwakelam.com/2020/07/08/renting-in-eighteenth-century-london/

- The school for self-defence for young ladies is entirely fictitious, although I like to think that such a thing could have existed.

- This story references a number of things which have happened before the start of this story.

   Most of those happened in earlier books in the Elbury Bouquet series, but some occurred in the His Majesty's Hounds series. So – the following paragraphs tell you where to find some of those things.

- If you would like to know more about the previous year's scandals in Lady Faith's family, you'll find that story in 'Restoring the Earl's Honour' (book 17 of His Majesty's Hounds).

- If you would like to know more about Mr Thomas Black, and how he came to be acknowledged by his half-brother, the Duke of Blackwater, you'll find that story in 'A Diamond for a Duke' (book 4 of The Elbury Bouquet), which will also give you more information about Thomas' aunt, Lady Prunella Danby, and why she was ostracised from society for twenty years.

- The first book in the Elbury Bouquet – 'A Spinster for a Spy', will give you information on how Trent came to marry Lily, and on how he came to 'work' for Lord Setford. There is a preview of that after the 'About the Author' section of this book.

- And as far as Lord Setford is concerned…. He is a major character in almost all of the His Majesty's Hounds books, and quite a few of the Elbury Bouquet books, but his personal story can be found in 'Attracting the Spymaster' (book 15 of the His Majesty's Hounds series).

My books tend to be very intertwined, even though each can be read as a standalone story. You will get the best reader experience if you read them in order – the His Majesty's Hounds series first, then the Elbury Bouquet Series. I have some more series coming which will also feature some familiar characters (the Duke of Traithewood's Legacy, and Lady Canterford's Conspirators, for a start), so keep an eye out for those over the coming months and years.

This has been the last book of the Elbury Bouquet series – I hope that you've enjoyed them all. If you have, please leave a review wherever you buy your books, or interact about books, so that others can find them and enjoy them too!

Regards

Arietta Richmond

ABOUT THE AUTHOR

Arietta Richmond has been a compulsive reader and writer all her life. Whilst her reading has covered an enormous range of topics, history has always fascinated her, and historical novels have been amongst her favourite reading.

She has written a wide range of work, from business articles and other non-fiction works (published under a pen name) but fiction has always been a major part of her life. Now, her Regency Historical Romance books are finally being released. The Derbyshire Set is comprised of 11 novels (9 released so far). The 'His Majesty's Hounds' series is comprised of 17 novels, with the last now released.

She also has a number of standalone novels released, and four other series of novels at various stages of release. She lives in Australia, and when not reading or writing, likes to travel, and to see in person the places where history happened.

Be the first to know about it when Arietta's next book is released! Sign up to Arietta's newsletter at

http://www.ariettarichmond.com

When you do, you will receive two free subscriber exclusive books - **'A Gift of Love',** which is a prequel to the Derbyshire Set series, and ends on the day that 'The Earl's Unexpected Bride' begins, and **'Madame's Christmas Marquis'** which is an additional story in the His Majesty's Hounds series.

These stories are not for sale anywhere – they are absolutely exclusive to newsletter subscribers!

Connect with Arietta:

Donate and support her on Kofi.com
https://ko-fi.com/ariettarichmondauthor

Follow her on Amazon - https://www.amazon.com/Arietta-Richmond/e/B016GG1KJ6/

Like her Facebook Page - https://www.facebook.com/AriettaRichmondAuthor

Follow her on Twitter - https://twitter.com/AriettaRichmond

Follow her on Instagram - https://www.instagram.com/AriettaRichmond/

Follow her on Bookbub – https://www.bookbub.com/authors/arietta-richmond

Follow her on Goodreads - https://www.goodreads.com/author/show/14508806.Arietta_Richmond

Here is your preview of

A SPINSTER FOR A SPY

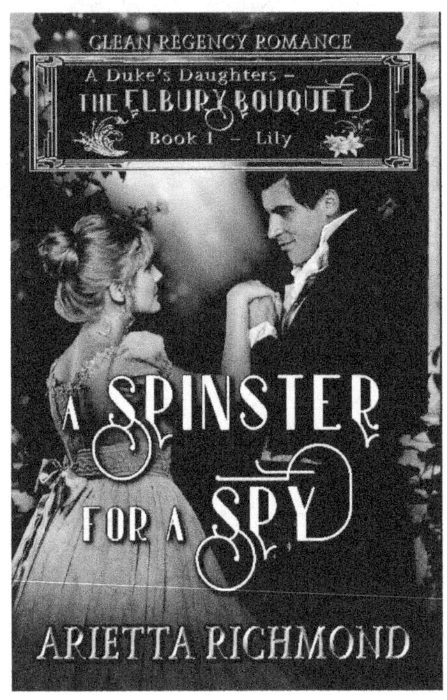

A Duke's Daughters –
The Elbury Bouquet - Book 1 - Lily

Arietta Richmond

CHAPTER ONE

"You, my dear sister, are a spinster. You cannot deny it any longer."

Thorne Gardenbrook, Marquess of Wildenhall, smiled smugly at his sister as he spoke.

"I am not a spinster! Certainly, I may be older than the age at which most girls marry… but I simply have not yet found a man that I care to marry."

Lady Lily Gardenbrook glared at her brother. He shook his head sadly.

"You delude yourself, Lily. You are two and twenty, and this will be your fourth Season – why do you not choose a man – it's not as if you have no suitors. I have introduced you to half the *ton*, in this last few years!"

"I do not choose any of them, because they are all horrible! They care nothing for me, for who I am – all they see is a Duke's daughter with a large dowry, and a figure which is not unappealing."

Thorne laughed, but his expression was serious when he spoke next.

"You may well be right, but I do not know that you can hope for the sort of love that our parents have – and you have been hoping for that, haven't you? Very few are lucky enough to marry someone that they love. And, in the end, better a marriage based on simple liking, than a lifetime alone and lonely."

"I have, indeed, been hoping for love. I am not sure that I could live with someone I barely liked – and most of the eligible men I don't like at all. If you are so sure that I should find someone this Season, then you had best introduce me to some new possibilities – for I refuse to contemplate those I already know."

Thorne frowned, and Lily knew that he truly did care what happened to her, and to all of her sisters. As brothers went, he was good – generally helpful, protective, and even willing to join in with mischief at times. And, though she would not admit it to him, he was right – she needed to act soon, to find a man to marry – for her sisters were not married either, and she suspected that they were holding back until Lily married. She sighed, and forced a smile onto her face. Thorne frowned again, shaking his head.

"I will try – but, truthfully, those you have not met are not of the kind of character that I would have my sister marry. Rakes, gamblers and fortune hunters make up a deplorable amount of society."

"Thank you - trying is all that either of us can do."

Thorne rose, and left the room.

Lily leant back into the embrace of the old armchair, staring blankly into the flickering flames in the grate before her. The book of poetry which she had been reading when Thorne came into the room still lay on her lap. Her fingers traced its cover, and her thoughts twisted in the never-ending circle that they had followed for three years now.

For there was more to her refusal of all suitors than simply the fact that none had inspired her to love. Her refusal was grounded in fear – a fear that her closely guarded secret would be discovered, that a husband would take from her the one thing which she most enjoyed. The thing which was, most certainly, not something which a lady of the *ton* could do, with the approval of society.

Trent Weatherton, Marquess of Canterford, inhaled deeply as he stepped through the door of Bigglesworth's Books.

There was something about the scent of books which spoke to his soul, which brought to mind winter afternoons ensconced in his library, by the fire, with a volume of poetry, or perhaps a history, or even, though he would not admit it to other gentlemen, a novel.

Mr Bigglesworth greeted him with a smile.

"Good day to ye, my Lord. I've a few volumes I think you'll like, if you've the time after your meeting?"

"Excellent, Bigglesworth – I always have the time for books."

Bigglesworth waved him past, and he slipped through the dusty curtain behind the counter, and into the dimness of the back corridor.

The rickety looking stairs were silent beneath his feet, as always, and the ancient looking door at the top was solid beneath his fingers. He knocked.

"Enter."

The room was everything that might not be expected. It was large, clean, and well lit by large glass windows all along one side. A rug of a quality which would not be out of place in a stately home graced the floor, and the couches that surrounded it were exquisitely carved and upholstered. The man who rose from one of them to greet him was of middling height, unremarkable except for his piercing grey eyes. Trent went forward to him.

"Lord Setford. I trust that your summons does not come due to bad news?"

"No, no. Nothing difficult this time, m'boy. Although you may not be enthusiastic about it. Do sit – the coffee is on the side table, if you've a mind to taste it."

"Your coffee is always worth drinking Lord Setford."

Trent sank onto the couch, and poured himself a cup of the strong bitter liquid from the pot that sat there.

He marvelled, again, at how Setford always managed to have perfect coffee waiting, no matter when a man arrived at his door.

"Good, Good. Now, let's to business. You understand the scope of the responsibilities you've been granted, I trust?"

"I do, if that is no more or less than you previously told me."

"It is. But what you may not have truly grasped, is the way in which you might best achieve what is needed."

"Oh?"

"Yes – if you thought that what I asked would allow you to avoid society events – as I know you've had a tendency to do for this last year and more, since your father's death – then you were mistaken. That's what I wanted to discuss today. If you are going to serve the Crown by managing and preventing civil unrest and treasonous activities within England, then you will need to be always gathering intelligence – not simply through the men I have assigned you, but yourself. For the greatest threats to England have as often come from amongst our own, as from abroad, and from amongst the aristocracy in particular. The poor rarely have the money or the time to stir up trouble, unlike our peers."

Trent studied Setford's face, wondering where this was going.

"I can see the truth in that. But... what do you want me to do? I freely admit that I am still learning the techniques which you so effortlessly apply."

Setford laughed, a full rich sound, and nodded.

"And that is exactly why I chose you, Canterford. You are willing to learn – you are astute, and observant – and that is exactly what I am asking you to act on. I need you to get about in society more, to become the man who is invited to all of the major hostesses' events, who is so well known that no one looks at him twice. For when you achieve that, you can move among them, observing everything, and no one will notice you doing so. If you get it right, half of them will even tell you their secrets voluntarily."

Trent sat for a moment, staring out of the windows at the rooftops of London, where dirtied snow slowly melted on soot covered slate. He took a deep breath and turned back to Setford.

"You, my Lord, are quite the most devious man I have ever met."

Setford laughed again, and gave a little seated bow.

"Glad you've realised that, m'boy."

"You know full well that if you had spoken of this requirement, when we first discussed me joining the ranks of the King's spies, I would likely have refused you. Instead you played upon my sense of duty, and my need to do something more than manage my estates, to move past my grief at my father's death. And now that I have fully committed to you, to serving the Crown in this way, you drop this upon me. I shudder at the very thought of endless evenings spent in the ballrooms and salons of London, eyed off, like a prime piece of horseflesh in the ring at Tattersall's, by all of those husband-hunting young women."

"Which is exactly why you are the right man for the job. You'll be focussed on what needs to be done, not on carousing and flirting." Trent winced, but nodded. Setford had the right of it, and he would not attempt to back away from the course he had committed to. Honour demanded that he be true to his word. "I will make it a little easier for you – I can guarantee you invitations from quite a few who also have some... relationship... to our work, to smooth your way into it. But it is up to you to appear as carefree as possible – like a man recently released from mourning who relishes the chance to go about in society."

"I can act the part, but I can't promise not to curse you in the privacy of my mind, if I find it all unutterably tedious!"

Setford laughed that hearty laugh again.

"I can't ask more than that m'boy – and who knows, you might even enjoy some of it."

Trent nodded, but his expression was dubious enough that it drew another laugh from Setford. Ruefully, he found himself laughing too.

"Did I really look that horrified by the idea?"

"You did, m'boy, you did."

"Well then, I will need to practise my dissembling, won't I? We can't have the hostesses of society realising just what I really think of their balls and soirees."

"You will indeed. And you can start tomorrow."

Setford lifted an embossed card from the table beside him, and passed it to Trent. Trent took it, hesitantly, as if it might bite, somehow. He felt, in that instant, as if something portentous would be started, simply by the act of reading that card. He shook the whimsical thought aside, and bent his eyes to the card.

> ***'The Duke and Duchess of Elbury would be pleased to welcome the Marquess of Canterford to a Soiree to be held at Elbury House.'***

The direction followed, and the stated date of the event was, as Setford had said, the following day.

"What did you tell them of me?"

Setford smiled.

"Very little – except that you are a friend, recently out of mourning, and wishing to re-establish himself in society. But Marcus, the Duke, no matter how genially blustering he may appear, is as astute as you are – he will understand that I have a purpose in assisting you with invitations, and he will also know not to ask. Just attend, observe, and try to enjoy yourself and look natural."

Trent could not prevent the snort of laughter that escaped him.

"Look natural? I have never, in my life, truly been comfortable amongst crowds of my peers – so perhaps natural is the wrong word. But I will try to look as if I actually want to be there."

CHAPTER TWO

Trent stepped down from the carriage and eyed the imposing home before him. Elbury House spoke of wealth, and prosperity, in every line of its façade. A number of other carriages drew up to set down their passengers as he made his way up the steps. He wondered just how large this soiree would be – it was only February, and the Season would not really begin for another month or so – yet it appeared that this might still be a fairly large event.

He drew a deep breath, his cravat suddenly feeling too tight. He could not hesitate. This was where the rest of his life began. Since his father's death, he had allowed himself to use mourning as an excuse – an excuse to not step out into society as 'the Marquess of Canterford' – to not discover if the cream of society thought him worthy to fill his father's place in the world.

That excuse was no longer available, and his commitment to the Crown, via Lord Setford, allowed him no further avoidance. Tonight, he would discover how they had judged him. He was not at all sure that he wanted to know.

He joined the receiving line, handing off his hat and outer coat to the waiting footman.

He was announced, and went forward to be greeted by the Duke and Duchess. The Duke was a kindly looking man, with greying hair that had once been a rich mahogany colour, of which traces remained. Trent bowed, and the Duke looked him up and down, then gave the tiniest nod.

"It's good to see you out and about, Canterford. Mourning saps the energy out of a man, after too long. Do let us know," here he inclined his head in the direction of his Duchess, who was smiling broadly, "if you'd like an introduction to anyone." He then indicated the young man standing at his other side. "Let's start that with an introduction to my son. Canterford, may I present Thorne Gardenbrook, Marquess of Wildenhall."

"Thank you, Your Grace. Wildenhall – I am pleased to make your acquaintance."

Trent moved on into the large parlour, where other guests milled about. It was not too crowded. Footmen circulated, offering drinks, and a small group of musicians played softly from a rather cramped spot in one corner of the room. He accepted a drink and looked about, desperately hoping to see someone whom he knew well enough to wish to talk to. That wish appeared to be in vain. Across the room, he saw a cluster of young women, who had enough of a similarity about their features that he concluded they must be sisters – most likely the Duke's daughters – there were seven of them, Setford had informed him.

Their hair varied in shade, from light blonde to a rich golden brown – all were beautiful, yet each distinctly different. He wondered what it would be like, to be part of such a large family.

The girls moved about, speaking to each other and to some of the guests, and he found himself idly watching as he sipped the wine in his hand. One of them turned, and he saw her face directly, for the first time. The noise around him faded away, and everything else seemed somehow less clear and sharp, as if the light from the chandelier above fell only upon that one woman.

He felt an odd rush of warmth through his body, and his breath came short. With difficulty, he dragged his eyes away from her.

What had just happened? He did not know, but he found that he needed the drink in his hand, needed to remind himself of the reason he was here, the reason that he would be attending so many more evenings like this. And that was to observe and listen, not to stand staring rudely at one of his host's daughters. He turned to watch the other side of the room, and nearly collided with Wildenhall.

"Canterford, there you are. The majority of the guests have finally arrived, and I have escaped the receiving line, thank God. I thought I'd find you, and follow through on that offer to introduce you around."

"I'd appreciate that. I was never much for city society, and then the year of mourning pulled me away from everything – I find that I am lamentably unaware of who is who and what the fads and fashions are."

"I doubt I can help with fads and fashions, but let me start by introducing you to my sisters. It's my official brotherly duty to introduce them to every eligible man in society." Trent must have winced a little, for Wildenhall laughed and went on, "I assure you, they are not your typical society misses."

"No? That sounds interesting – what makes them different?"

"A grim determination to do things their way, regardless of what society expects. And far more intelligence than is regarded as suitable in a woman. If they ever all agree on something, they are a force to be reckoned with. But never fear, the chances of them all agreeing are slim."

His words startled Trent to laughter, which he quickly repressed. They reached the cluster of young women, and Trent wondered at their ages – for all seven of them to be there, the youngest could not be less than fifteen, which would make the eldest over twenty – a highly unusual age for an unmarried woman of good breeding who was possessed of a sizeable dowry. He pushed the consideration aside, as Wildenhall launched into introductions.

"Sisters, allow me to introduce you to the Marquess of Canterford. Canterford, these are my sisters – Lady Lily, Lady Hyacinth, Lady Rose, Lady Camellia, Lady Primrose, Lady Violet, and Lady Iris."

Wildenhall indicated each one as he spoke their name, and Trent dutifully bowed to each. But his mind was a jumble after the very first one – for Lady Lily was the woman whose beauty had so stopped everything around him, when he had sighted her across the room. That he even managed to respond politely to the others astounded him. They each considered him with curious eyes, and he felt self-conscious – how did they perceive him? Did they think him a fortune hunter, or worse? Lady Lily spoke first.

"Lord Canterford – It is a pleasure to see a new face – society can become so dull after a while!"

Her voice was soft, melodious, yet very clear and carrying. A voice which would do equally well with singing, or with conversation, and not tire the ear of the person listening. Lady Hyacinth nodded her agreement.

"A pleasure indeed, my Lord – and a pity that there is not to be dancing this evening, for a new possibility for a dance partner holds great appeal."

Lady Hyacinth's voice was sharper, and held an edge of intended cynicism. Her words were bold and forward, yet her smile defused that, and left him wondering if he had imagined the edge to it. Lady Lily cast a glance sideways at her sister, and pursed her lips a moment. So, he was not the only one to detect that edge. He felt the need to respond, and for a moment a desperate fear filled him – he simply was not good at this social banter! But Setford's face rose in his mind, calmly believing that he, Trent, could do this, and he swallowed.

"A pity indeed, Ladies, although, perhaps, an advantage for me – for should I be called upon to dance with each and every one of you, as of a certainty I would be, for it would be rude to do otherwise – I fear that I might suffer exhaustion by the end of the evening."

They laughed at his words, and he felt a little better – until he caught Lady Lily's eye. Her expression told him, quite clearly, that pretty words meant nothing to her, and that, perhaps, his riposte had reduced him in her estimation. He found that an unpalatable realisation – he did not wish to be poorly regarded by Lady Lily.

<<<<O>>>>

Lily was finding the evening surprisingly dull – she had looked forward to it, as a taste of the Season to come, but it was less than thrilling – the same faces, the same conversations, even much the same gossip. Until the moment when her brother appeared beside her, with a man she had never seen before.

When she had suggested that Thorne should introduce her to some eligible men that she had not previously met, she had not expected him to manage to do so – for he had been right in his comment that many of the possibilities, if not all, were rakes and wastrels. Yet here he was, barely a day later, achieving the impossible. The man beside him was tall, with dark, almost mahogany toned glossy hair, undeniably good-looking, yet not ostentatiously so. His attire was elegant, understated, perfectly tailored. But when Thorne introduced him, what caught her attention most was his eyes, which met hers as he bowed over her hand. They were the shade that was often referred to as hazel – a gold-green-brown tone, that seemed to shift with the light. Bright shimmering gold flecks swam in their depths.

For a moment, everything else seemed to fade away – the sounds in the room diminished, and she felt flustered, uncertain. Yet he had done nothing but bow, perfect in his politeness. Then the spell was broken, and he moved on to greeting her sisters, as Thorne introduced each of them. Once the introductions were finished, there was a moment of awkward silence, in which Thorne looked pointedly at Lily. She flushed a little – his meaning was clear – here, as promised, was a new man for her to consider – she should at least attempt to converse with him! But words seemed to have deserted her – what could she say to this man, who so disconcerted her?

"Lord Canterford – It is a pleasure to see a new face – society can become so dull after a while!"

She was horrified at how clumsy her words sounded, but they were spoken. Thorne raised an eyebrow at her, obviously wondering what had caused his normally articulate sister to deliver such a poor conversational opening.

Lord Canterford was obviously uncertain how to respond, and as he hesitated, Hyacinth, in her usual bold manner, spoke up.

"A pleasure indeed, my Lord – and a pity that there is not to be dancing this evening, for a new possibility for a dance partner holds great appeal."

Lily almost winced, only just managing to stay absolutely still. Why, Hyacinth had, with those words, almost demanded that, at the first opportunity, Lord Canterford ask her to dance! Lily found that the prospect of Lord Canterford dancing with Hyacinth did not please her. Silence fell again, and Lily turned her gaze back to Lord Canterford, curious – what could he possibly say in response? And would it be simply polite, or would it be flirting and flattering? Would his words reveal his character to be no different from all of the rest of the unappealing men available to her? An odd expression flitted across his face – one she could not interpret, then he spoke.

"A pity indeed, Ladies, although, perhaps, an advantage for me – for should I be called upon to dance with each and every one of you, as of a certainty I would be – for it would be rude to do otherwise – I fear that I might suffer exhaustion by the end of the evening."

Lily looked away, her heart sinking. Flattery, almost flirtation. So – he was no different from all of the others. She had hoped... but it seemed not. Thorne would just have to try again. Still, perhaps she should not completely discount Lord Canterford yet – that fleeting expression intrigued her.

They spoke for a little longer, and Lily, later, could not remember a word of what was said, beyond the fact that he was polite even to the youngest of her sisters, who was rather flustered by that fact. Then, as was appropriate, Thorne led Lord Canterford away, moving about the room, introducing him to other guests.

Lily's eyes followed him – she seemed unable to prevent herself from watching. Once the evening was over, she would have many questions for Thorne – who, really, was Lord Canterford? Why had she never seen him before? What did Thorne think of his character?

The compulsion to know all that she could of the man surprised her, and she shook her head in annoyance, dragging her eyes away from him, and turning back to her sisters.

"Taken with him, are you?"

Hyacinth's tone was sharp, amused, and Lily gritted her teeth a moment before replying sweetly.

"No more than you are, dear sister, if your bold suggestion of dancing is any indicator."

"Ha! What was I to do, after your terrible conversational beginning? And at least I did not stand there making calf eyes at the man. Still, we must agree – any new man is worth considering, if any of us are ever to find husbands we can stand to spend our lives with."

Iris and Violet stared at their eldest sisters, their faces a little shocked at the discussion, then turned away, giggling together. The rest of her sisters ignored the whole thing, all but Camellia, whose response was as cheerful and hopeful as always.

"He did seem quite nice, Lily, if rather quiet. Perhaps he is not used to large families. Did you truly like him? It would be wonderful if you did – surely you will find a man worth loving soon."

"Oh Camellia, you are ever the optimist. We have only just met him – how can I possibly know, yet, if I like him?"

"Well... I rather think that you might know, if he is truly the man for you. Bella says that she knew, from the first moment that she saw Lucian. Even if he took rather a long time to realise..."

Lily laughed lightly – Camellia's view of love had been coloured by the recent wedding of her best friend, Miss Isabella Morton, who was now the Duchess of Hartswood. But her sister's words did make her think – there had been that odd moment, when she had first looked into Lord Canterford's eyes... could that mean anything? She was not sure at all.

And then the thought rose in her mind – even if she did like him, was he a man who could accept her secret?

Trent felt, as Wildenhall led him across the room, away from the sisters, as if he was waking from a terrifying dream. He could barely remember a word that had been spoken, the swirl of cheerful young women had dazzled and confused him. Having grown up with just one sister, the large family overwhelmed.

What was still clear in his mind was the momentary look of disappointment on Lady Lily's face, when he had made that reply to her sister, about dancing. What was it that had so displeased her in what he had said? For a moment, it had transported him back to the moments in his childhood, when his father had shaken his head sadly, as if Trent could never measure up to his father's hopes.

He pushed that thought aside. His father was gone. He was no longer that boy. And by his commitment to the Crown, by accepting the tasks that Lord Setford offered, he had set himself on a path where he had no choice but to succeed, no matter how many people he disappointed in the process. But that look upon her face had hurt. For some reason, her opinion of him mattered – a great deal.

Read the rest at:

https://ariettarichmond.com/go/get-a-spinster-for-a-spy

BOOKS IN THE A DUKE'S DAUGHTERS – THE ELBURY BOUQUET SERIES

BOOKS IN THE HIS MAJESTY'S HOUNDS SERIES

BOOKS IN THE DERBYSHIRE SET

The Earl's Unexpected Bride

The Captain's Compromised Heiress

The Viscount's Unsuitable Affair

The Count's Impetuous Seduction

The Rake's Unlikely Redemption

The Marquess' Scandalous Mistress

The Marchioness' Second Chance

A Viscount's Reluctant Passion

Lady Theodora's Christmas Wish

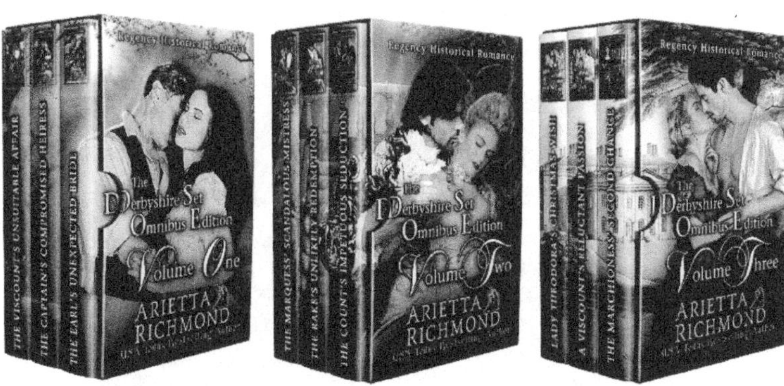

The Derbyshire Set Omnibus Edition Vol. 1 (the first three books all in one)

The Derbyshire Set Omnibus Edition Vol. 2 (the second three books all in one)

The Derbyshire Set Omnibus Edition Vol. 3 (the third three books all in one)

BOOKS IN THE REGENCY SCANDALS SERIES

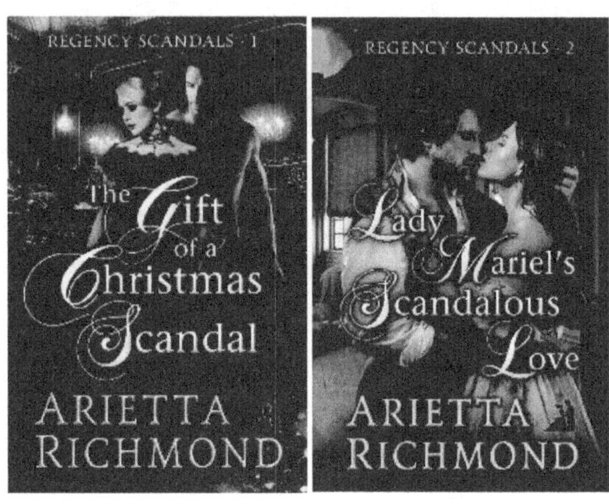

BOOKS IN THE NETTLEFOLD CHRONICLES

REGENCY COLLECTIONS WITH OTHER AUTHORS

BOOKS IN THE REGENCY GOTHIC SERIES

THE HER DUKE COLLECTION

THEMED REGENCY COLLECTIONS

OTHER BOOKS FROM ARIETTA

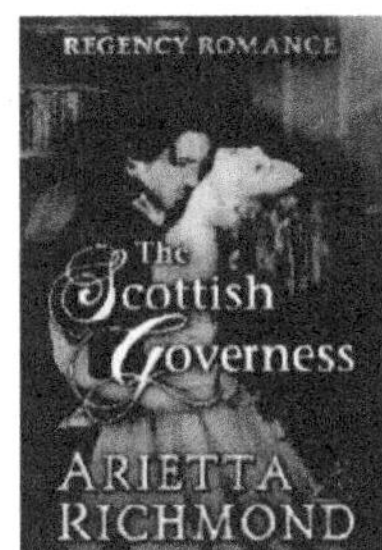

REGENCY COLOURING BOOKS

More coming soon!

OTHER BOOKS FROM DREAMSTONE PUBLISHING

230

Dreamstone publishes books in a wide variety of categories ranging from Clean Romance to Erotica, to Kids Books, Books on Writing, Business Books, Photography, Cook Books, Diaries, Colouring books and much more. New books are released each month.

Be the first to know when our next books are coming out

Be first to get all the news – sign up for our newsletter at

http://www.dreamstonepublishing.com